LIPSTICK EYEBROWS

LIPSTICK EYEBROWS

HONNO MODERN FICTION

First published in Great Britain in 2023 by Honno Press
D41, Hugh Owen Building, Aberystwyth University, Ceredigion, SY23 3DY

1 2 3 4 5 6 7 8 9 10

Copyright: The Contributors 2023

The right of The Contributors to be identified as the Author of the Work has been asserted in accordance with the Copyright, Designs and Patents Act 1988. All rights reserved. No part of the book may be reproduced, stored in a retrieval system, or transmitted in any form, or by any means, electronic, mechanical, photocopying, recording or otherwise without the prior permission of the copyright owner.

A catalogue record for this book is available from the British Library.

Published with the financial support of the Books Council of Wales.

ISBN 978-1-912905-90-4 (paperback)
ISBN 978-1-912905-91-1(ebook)
Cover design: Ifan Bates
Text design: Elaine Sharples
Printed by: 4Edge Limited

This is a work of fiction and no resemblance to persons living or dead is intended or implied.

Contents

Introduction	1
By the Water's Edge *Silvia Rose*	5
To Buy an Expensive Dream *Chinyere Chukwudi-Okeh*	13
Wild Romances *Kate Waddon*	25
The King of the Fairies *Carolyn Thomas*	33
Summer's End *Gosia Buzzanca*	45
Lipstick Eyebrows *Naomi Paulus*	57
Scab *Ellen Davies*	71
Something about Weddings *Julie Primon*	81
Pearls Before Swine *Tracey Rhys*	91

Author Biographies

Editor Biographies

Introduction

Honno has been dedicated to publishing the works of women from and residing in Wales exclusively for nearly 40 years. We are proud to be the UK's longest running women's press. There is no other publisher committed to lifting and celebrating the voices of Welsh women. Our entire list proudly celebrates the culture of women in Wales and beyond.

However, we are acutely aware that we are living in a world where the thoughts and opinions of women are still overlooked; and women are still being objectified, scrutinised and abused. So many girls worldwide are still not getting an education. I cannot imagine my own daughter not being able to attend school. But even in the UK, I am aware that she will still have to fight hard to create her own space, she will still be vulnerable when walking alone; she will still experience sexism: sexism, which begins at school age with things such as princess parties for girls and superhero parties for boys, and the belief that only girls should wear dresses and trousers are only for boys.

This anthology was a chance for us at Honno to continue our legacy of elevating the voices of women, creating a space for creativity, narrative and experience. So many of us come to writing under adverse and difficult conditions: we carve a space in the corner of the kitchen, at the end of a long day at work, in the midnight hours nursing babies, catch a moment whilst children are at school; or jotting down a thought whilst waiting with an elderly loved one in the hospital or doctor's surgery. The title story 'Lipstick Eyebrows' so tenderly explores female dignity and care, setting the tone for our ambition for the book. It is compassion for each other that makes our community thrive and drives change for the better. And women will always continue to write. Women write everywhere and anywhere. We are good at that. And we are good at adapting to adversity.

While reading the many stories submitted for this anthology, it became clear to us how varied and vast the experiences of Welsh women truly are today. Women residing in, or originally from, Wales have a diverse range of histories, backgrounds and cultures from which to draw their tales.

Each of the stories chosen invites the reader into a strange new world, giving us a glimpse into the varied experiences of Welsh women, from those that paddle in Italian lakes to those that find peace at a wedding ceremony. Ultimately, the stories chosen are stories concerned with liminal spaces – there are service stations, cruise ships, airports and hospital beds. Throughout the collection, people arrive and depart. Much like the women of Wales, the characters in this book are in a perpetual state of flux – on the cusp of adulthood, entering new relationships, learning new ways of viewing the world.

Introduction

An unnamed woman is desperate to escape the monotony of her day-to-day life, searching for her own *Wild Romances* in Kate Waddon's story. With an incompetent husband and three dependent children, who can blame her for searching for a little excitement? Will she find it if she leaves the service station, or will the road always lead her straight back home? In Carolyn Thomas' story, two young girls learn that the woods are full of secrets, including *The King of the Faeries* himself. But what will the rest of the family members make of this chance encounter? It's the 90s in Poland, the Princess is dead, the Hanson Brothers dominate magazine covers, and a new school term is about to begin in *Summer's End*, but Kasia will be taking more than a new school uniform with her come September. Gosia Buzzanca tells the story of a girlhood stripped away too soon. *By the Water's Edge* in rural Bosnia, a young girl embraces her discomfort, casting aside her gut instinct in an attempt to impress an older man. Amongst the sweat and heat, the comforting heap of pancakes, and the laughs that come like 'claps of thunder,' there is something deeply disturbing about trainee policeman Atso. Silvia Rose deftly weaves this coming-of-age tale with beautiful imagery and a self-sure narrative. Julie Primon proves there is *Something About Weddings* when Claire strikes up a conversation with Sandra, her ex-boyfriend's new wife. Perhaps she was right to leave her partner at home, after all. When the house phone in Naomi Paulus' *Lipstick Eyebrows* rings in the dead of night, it could only be 'Little Ears', the nursing home's night manager. In this darkly humorous story, a young woman travels across her hometown to the bedside of her dying grandmother. Navigating this familiar landscape, through memories of her past and family history, forces her to reconcile where she has come from with where she is going. *Pearls Before Swine* by Tracey Rhys sees a couple in their later years getting to know each other whilst enjoying a cruise. When Evelyn finds a pearl in her dinner one evening, it brings her even closer to handsome Gio. This is a story of a woman reclaiming herself, her sense of adventure, her sexuality and her life. In Ellen Davies' story set in the Welsh valleys, Caryl travels home for her estranged mother's funeral. While trying to reconcile with her brother and sister-in-law, a *Scab* is picked away – but will it reveal a fleshy wound, or a scar? In *To Buy an Expensive Dream*, a flight that will lead to a new life is about to depart ... but will our protagonist be on board? Chinyere Chukwudi-Okeh's tale of travel hinges on the dissonance that can occur when reality does not meet our expectations.

Selecting these stories and working closely with their authors has been a privilege, and we are sure you, the reader, will enjoy discovering these contemporary voices as much as we have.

Rebecca Parfitt
Commissioning Editor
Honno Press

Mari Ellis Dunning
Anthology Co-Editor

By the Water's Edge

by Silvia Rose

I left the boxy flat with my family squeezed inside – my mother sweating by the window, her unshaved legs spread apart in a warrior position; my grandma sweating by the stove, dipping a finger into the bubbling soup, licking it off with a click; my brother and sister bored and hot and sweating on the sofa.

I was sweating, my thighs already sticky as they rubbed against themselves under my skirt. I called back through the closed door, 'Just going for a swim!'

I walked down the steps that echoed and smelt like every other hallway in this place – a mixture of cigarettes and stock-cubes. The plastic bag I carried sliced into my hand, weighed down with a towel, picnic supplies, and a book I hadn't started yet. It was too hot to eat or read but I needed the pretence of having something to do.

Outside, the air was heavy, basting me with greasy heat. Moving was hard and slow. I waited by the road while a tractor passed, wheezing like an old pair of lungs. The farmer waved and beeped his horn.

Remembering the way to the riverbank, I crossed over to the dirt-track lined with unfinished houses on either side. Some were crumbling, clearly destroyed, others were half-built and caged by scaffolding. The grass was dead and yellow, the mud grey and dry. On my right was Mira's house, a friend of my grandma's who we'd visited the previous day. I passed the shady patch of garden where we had sat eating watermelon and held her baby granddaughter, all dressed in white.

Children played in the field ahead, kicking balls through rusty white goalposts stuck in at jaunty angles. Children half-naked, skinny and brown and bare-footed. They ran and screamed at each other. I felt embarrassed, like they were looking at me knowing I didn't belong, that perhaps they could smell my Britishness.

I walked to the quiet patch by the river, away from the wooden jetty where the dogs played and left their mess to slip on. Through the gaps in the trees I could see the broad stretch of water, glinting and playful.

Cornfields spread out to my left, so tall I felt protected. Grassy mounds and weeping trees surrounded the riverbank, soft and swamp-like. There was noise – hot noise – bugs and echoes of the children screaming. I lay on my towel feeling self-conscious even though I was alone. I straightened it out, moved it so it was level on the ground and wondered which way I should put my head. The towel was starchy and coarse on my back. I stripped down to my bikini and sat bent over, kneading the folds of my stomach. I lay down instead, preferring it flat.

I lay with my hands above my head and gave my body a stretch right down to the toes and I felt it in me, some fleshy heat that travelled up and through me, collecting at my dewy navel. With my eyes closed I felt drowsy, drugged. It was only half-pleasant.

Out of nowhere, the ground vibrated with a thud. I tensed up; my eyes still closed. The thudding stopped and I felt the sunlight blocked out from beneath my eyelids.

'*Čao.*'

It was a voice that resounded, stayed static in the air.

I started, sat up, twisted around awkwardly. It was Atso, Mira's son. I'd only met him in passing, dressed in his light-blue uniform buttoned all the way to the top. Tight trousers. He had smiled down at me, my head only reaching the badge on his chest. My mother had told me he was training to be a policeman.

Now he was standing there, towering over me even more. He wore swimming trunks, white and worn. He had foam slippers on his feet. One of them was almost touching my hand, which was spread out to support my weight.

'*Čao*', I answered back, the only word I could pronounce with confidence.

He crouched down, a violent and sudden action, changing his whole stature. His elbows leant on knees that jutted out towards me. He squinted through the sun and smiled wide. There were small gaps between his teeth.

'Is hot.' The words shivered and wafted in the space between us.

'Yeah.'

He came to sit beside me, I moved over on my towel. I hugged my knees as close as I could. His shoulder brushed mine so lightly I could feel a map of nerves run beneath my skin. He opened his mouth – closed it again – furrowed his eyebrows.

'Uhh ... you swim?'

I unclasped my knees.

'Yeah.'

'*Aide.*'

He stood up, his knee next to my head now, hairs like brambles.

I waited until he had walked right down to the riverbank. I was suspended for a moment – I wondered if it was a joke, if he really wanted me here. He hadn't brought a towel. I watched as he kicked off his slippers and without a backwards glance jumped into the water. He howled like a wolf. The sound shocked me out of my stupor in time to see his face rising out and sparkling. I smiled.

'*Aide!*' he called again.

I snapped the fabric of my bikini bottoms, pulling them to cover my buttocks. The earth under my feet was smooth and compact. I didn't jump. I stepped in slowly, my blood fizzing with the cold. He laughed when I threw myself under and resurfaced with a scream.

The river was like a lake – so wide and still. The water was cloudy and filtered green from the bordering trees. I could feel the promise of river weeds tickling my toes as I kicked lazily to keep afloat. Atso did flips underwater. I swam breaststroke, wondering if I looked elegant or just shy.

There was a moment when I turned around and he was gone. I looked in all directions. Then I felt a tug on my ankle. Something was pulling me under. I struggled to get away – splashed and breathed in gulps of water. Then he emerged beside me, hair dripping, an intent smile coursing over his face. I splashed him.

'*Nemoj*! Don't do that!' I said, laughing.

We swam for hours until the water felt lukewarm and natural, like air around our bodies. The river had soaked off a layer of skin. I felt opened up and stretched out.

We spoke through laughter and exclamations of 'Ahhh…' The sky was pink and alive – a final burst of colour before nightfall. I followed Atso as he swam to the shore, watched his shoulder blades beat like wings.

It was strange when we stood on dry land. Everything was heavier and more real. I handed him my towel and pretended to search through my bag. I couldn't look at him as he rubbed his hair dry. The way he bent down reminded me of grazing bulls.

We walked in twilight, his slippers slapping his feet, a rhythm conducting the near silence. Then he asked, 'How many years you have?'

I hesitated. Two slaps of the slippers.

'Fourteen,' I replied, immediately wishing I'd added on three years instead of one. He turned to me, his eyes white, '*Strašno!*' Then he laughed low and long and said something I didn't understand.

The dirt-track was lit up by kitchen lights, cosy and orange. There were still people outside in their gardens, stoking mini-bonfires and roasting corn; an old man loading firewood into the back of his truck.

'*Jesi li gladno?* Eat?' Atso asked, stopping outside the bare-brick walls of his mother's house. Half his face was in shadow, making his long nose stick out and his features look moulded like clay. I nodded, feeling my skin prickle. I followed him inside where Mira was at the sink, her body bulky, the same formidable stance as my grandma. Her face lit up when she saw us. She came to me and kissed my cheeks, said my name in a throaty voice. She spoke no English but I laughed along regardless. When we were here the day before she had sneaked glasses of *rakija* to my little brother until we realised, as he rushed around, crashing his head on the sofa, that he was drunk.

I sat down at the table, which was covered in a plastic sheet, decorated with gingham and cartoon woodland animals. The news was on the TV. I could make out a shot of some smoke-filled city before it switched to a 'turbo-folk' concert. Trashy ballads filled the room.

Mira poured me a glass of strawberry juice, thick and pulpy, ice-cold from the fridge. Atso laid down a plate piled high with ready-made pancakes and next to it, a tub of chocolate spread so big it could have held paint. Still topless, he sat down beside me, stray pearls of river water dripping down his temples. We ate in silence while Mira fussed around us. The pancakes were damp with butter. I could feel the wet bikini soak my clothes.

Atso motioned me to eat more – I refused. He laughed and said something about 'little' and 'English'. Mira laughed back and placed a parched hand on my shoulder.

It was nearly eight. I wondered if my brother and sister were in bed; if my mother was also looking at the clock. I discarded the thought when Atso invited me upstairs, leading me along an olive-green carpet. First, he showed me his brother's bedroom. It was bare apart from a mattress on the floor. He tried to explain where he'd gone. The walls were painted a bright, sickly blue, covered with graffiti letters in shades of silver and gold. Some words I recognised, 'Gangsta', 'Get Money Fuck Bitchez', dollar signs everywhere. There was a sort of pride in the way Atso showed me the walls.

His room was next door. It was white and just as bare. His bed had a frame at least.

A red leather punch-bag hung in the corner, swaying from the slam of the door.

He pulled on a t-shirt. It was plain, grey-blue, too big even for him. He sat on a plastic chair while I sat on the bed, leaning against the wall, my legs rigid and straight on top of the duvet. The laptop made a welcoming ping as he turned it on.

'You watch video?'

'*Da*.'

He clicked on a folder and scrolled down, muttering under his breath. He showed me videos, some I'd seen before, of kids falling off skateboards, football tackles gone wrong, singers tripping onstage. He made me jump with his laughter; it burst out of him like claps of thunder.

Then he showed me something else.

It was a man sitting at a table, filmed like a police tape, grainy and official. The man was crying, pleading. I didn't recognise the language. There was another, deeper voice coming from behind the camera. The man's eyes were dark and laced with desperation. Saliva trickled down the corners of his mouth.

Then – a gunshot.

The man's head crashed and spluttered, a mess of red on the wall behind. It all happened in an instant. Then the video ended.

Atso was laughing. A jolt ran through me. I tried to look relaxed and push out a giggle but I felt sick with adrenalin. I worried that he could hear my pulse – so loud, it was as if the blood wanted to escape my body.

He sighed; exhausted, amused.

'*Ace Ventura*? Jim Carrey?'

I nodded. My hands held each other still.

He played the film and turned off the light. For the next hour and a half, I felt his body next to mine like a radiator turned up too high.

I knew my mother would be worried by the time he walked me home. We were surrounded by the creaks of crickets and the warm residue of the day. All the houses were dark by now, drenched in blue ink. I wrapped my arms around myself, the jumper he'd leant me scratchy, almost reaching my knees.

We walked slowly. Atso dragged his feet, kicking the dust and stones. He kept his eyes forward like they were stuck.

I thought I could see my grandma's balcony on the far side of the road. White sheets hung high on the washing line. I heard a window close and the distant sound of a dog's bark.

'You cold?' he asked, as I shivered.

To Buy an Expensive Dream

by Chinyere Chukwudi-Okeh

Murtala Mohammed International Airport Nigeria, 6 PM

A siren is blaring at the entrance of the airport, waiting to receive a dignitary or VIP, as your people prefer to say, as though *dignitary* cannot carry the import of a person. Dignitary sounds too smooth, almost banal, giving no room for emphasis; unlike VIP. VIP: affricate-vowel-plosive, lots of room for emphasis, allowing for your people's penchant for aggrandisement.

Not too far from the VIP people is an ambulance waiting to receive a corpse returning from the diaspora. As one group stands by their convoy with flags of solidarity and chants of praise, the others are mostly in black, somnolent, waiting for their dead. Among them is a young woman who sits by herself, crying quietly. She is pregnant, you can see. Perhaps, it is her husband who is being returned home in a non-descript box. The others, with posters of the dead, give voice to their grief.

'Paulinus!'
'Chai! Paulo!'
'Why do you have to die in a foreign land?'

The men among the group snap their fingers and shrug off their grief.

You watch men with guns come close and start pointing wordlessly towards the car park. You understand that the soldier is telling them to move, because there is no traffic allowed at the entrance of the airport, and neither death nor status will receive an exception to this rule.

The jubilant group is boisterous. They intone the name of their candidate: Honourable Danshiki of the Alliance for Wealth Party. They are all clad in Ankara and tarpaulin clothes bearing his face and party symbol.

Tiny beads of sweat shine on the faces of the mourners and mingle with tears as they stand by the hearse. An elderly woman drops to the ground, wailing uncontrollably as the crowd surrounds her.

'My son. My only son! Who will comfort me? Pauli, you were supposed to bury me. Who will cover my face? *Eeeeeeeeewu*!'

Now covered by patches of wet sand from rolling on the wet ground, her Ankara wrapper comes undone, revealing a white satin underskirt. The consolers gather around her and try to hold the wrapper in place, all the while sniffing back their own grief and wiping off their snot and sweat. The soldiers look on, stoic, as though saying, *we have seen these before. Move, damn it!*

A cloud has been gathering all day, and the airport lounge seems like a bubble about to burst. From the planes in the waiting terminals to the people rushing to be flown in them, everything and everyone moves swiftly. The rain starts falling in rhythmic *toh-toh-toh* before losing its rhythm and falling in a heavy torrent. Only the thunder can be heard as people trudge to the terminal with their luggage in tow, leaving wet trails behind. The cacophony of vendors selling padlocks, bottled water, pure water, bags, boxes, and cybercafé agents calling on travellers to pay and fill their passenger locator forms can be heard.

Everywhere you look, you see the effect of Covid-19. Stringent measures have been introduced around the airport; everyone is wearing a face mask; every door has an automatic sanitizer dispenser. What you notice the most, however, is that everyone – airlines, immigration officers, padlock sellers, and cybercafés – has found a way to make money from the process.

You and Uba dash out of your overheated Toyota Sienna to defy the gridlock caused by the joint effort of the mourners and praise singers. You rush through the organised chaos at the entrance and along the hallway. You move quickly. It's the reason you wore your most comfortable pair of blue jeans, white sneakers and a grey sweatshirt. You reach for a bottle of water from one of the water vendors but change your mind in favour of a cheaper option, *pure water*, squeezing a crumpled ten naira note into the impatient vendor's hand. You and Uba drag your travel boxes along the wet, slippery floor of the airport. You start making your way to the British Airways checkpoint and join the queue of disgruntled travellers lamenting the different ills bedevilling the country and how the airport has become a circus.

'I am not happy, Uba. Imagine spending hours in traffic, in this heat, driving from the Island to the Mainland, only to be beaten by the rain at the airport,' you say.

'But that is normal, Mma,' Uba says, placing a hand on your shoulder.

'No! It's not normal that the first thing I see in this airport is a group of people in black crying for their dead family member.'

'Well, I first saw the group in colourful clothes, singing for their party leader, and that is a good omen,' Uba says.

You cast a sardonic look at him, your husband who chooses to only see the good in every situation. He draws you into a hug, and details of your lovemaking every day for the past week start to sneak into your mind. You made love in every room of your house, twisting yourself into every Kamasutra pose your weight allowed. Last night's lovemaking felt particularly urgent. You clawed at his back extra tight, and he pushed into you a little bit harder, deeper, lasting longer than all the other nights. When, after you had an orgasm in the middle of another orgasm, he came; you cried and laughed at the same time. You hoped it would be enough. Now, at the airport, you push the memories back and save them for cold and lonely days ahead.

'It doesn't matter what you see here at the airport. The future is Welsh, baby. In a few hours you will be in Wales. Focus on the beauties of your destination.'

'Beauties? C'mon Uba! Wales doesn't even get enough snow,' you reply.

'Then that means less cold for you. Focus on the positives, dear. You are making me nervous,' Uba replies, and moves faster towards the counter as you hurry behind him.

You are the forerunner who is travelling ahead to water the ground of your family's dream of relocating to the UK. You chose the education route to the United Kingdom, just like half of the country now assembled at the airport.

As Uba opens the boxes, rearranging the contents to confuse the scale, you think of your four children and how you will survive without them; fresh tears roll down your cheeks. Uba stares at you in disbelief.

'Mma, what is this now? Would you rather we stay back and be roasted to death by these terrorists or killed for our inability to pay ransom if we get kidnapped? Or perhaps we should fold our hands and wait for trigger-happy policemen to locate us with their 'stray' bullets? C'mon sweetheart, cheer up and...'

'I will miss my children. I don't care about kidnappers and terrorists. Keep my children safe 'til you join me in December. Keep a close eye on Chikaima, nothing must happen to her. The uncertainty of this arrangement is killing me. I wish we could all travel together and not in batches.' You pull out a handkerchief and wipe your reddened face. 'And we have so much debt.'

Uba speaks; he is forceful. 'Whoever wants to harm my children must face me first, and I never lose a fight. This is a perfect plan, and everything will fall in place. As for the debts, when we start earning in pounds, servicing naira debts will be piecemeal. Trust me, my love.'

You nod, wiping your face to dry your tears. You and your husband have borrowed a fortune to make this relocation happen. You sold land, electronics, furniture, gold, jewellery, your wedding gown, and even your wedding rings to fund your visa fees. You remember that hot afternoon when you both took some of your household items to a thrift shop in Oshodi. The buyer had agreed to buy at the advertised rate but succeeded in taking every item lower than the agreed price. You had carried all the items to his shop and could not return home with them.

'I will buy you a better ring once we clear our debts and stabilise in the UK,' Uba told you on the day you sold your rings. You smiled and happily emptied your meagre savings and converted valuables. Your once heavily-decorated and furnished apartment has been reduced to one wardrobe, a flat mattress with two pillows and a mat.

Uba doesn't mind using the mat while the children sleep on the mattress.

You bring out a list of your debts and pray in your heart that this journey is worth it.

An old woman trudges towards your queue, tired from shuttling her boxes. She stops to catch her breath. She is dressed in immaculate white lace and a lacey head wrap. She wears white open-toe sandals that reveal well-manicured toenails, and a red handbag that complements her clothes. Her accessories shine like little stars. The desperate shuffling and ruffling of travellers and immigration officers do not stop around her and she momentarily loses her balance and catches herself mid-way, steadying her buckling knees from falling forward.

Uba moves and you frown. You know his disposition to lend a helping hand to everyone around him, but this is neither the place nor time to be focused on anyone but you. He stops and looks at you for approval, a plea in his eyes. You fix him a stern gaze and he stands transfixed to the spot, casting a helpless glance at the old lady. In the past weeks, he has taken loans and almost sold the clothes on his back to raise the money for your ticket. He has gone above and beyond, so you think that perhaps you should not deny him this chance to do a good deed for someone else, to soothe his own soul. You nod, giving him the all-clear.

'I'll be right back, I promise,' he says, and dashes off. He approaches the old lady, all smiles; he bows slightly and extends his hands towards her. 'Mama don't worry, I will help you,' he says to the old lady. He helps her carry her luggage for weighing – two large, shiny, plastic boxes and a luxurious silver-coloured hand suitcase. You can see clearly now that the red bag is a fancy Louis Vuitton. After the verification process and transfer of the big boxes, Uba urges you to keep an eye on the old lady throughout the journey and help her with her hand luggage.

'My son, is that your wife?' The old lady asks.

'Yes ma,' he says, smiling. You are actually proud of him for having the presence of mind to help a senior citizen in the middle of all the chaos, even if you are mildly annoyed.

The old lady holds both of you by hand. 'I want to pray for you,' she says. Uba smiles and casts you a side glance. He believes that the words of elders are potent and travel from their lips straight to God's ears. He bows his head and you do too, but you do not close your eyes.

'My God will surprise you two. As you have given thought to the plight of an old woman, God will shock you beyond words. You will receive a miracle so great that every ear that hears it will tingle. This act of kindness will open doors for your family,' she says, suppressing an urge to cry. As she releases her hands, she wipes her face with a white handkerchief. She bore the weight of her luggage on a bad knee, to avoid missing her flight.

You say 'Amen'. Uba's amen is markedly higher than yours. Uba hugs you tightly, telling you the new land will treat you well.

'Wales will open doors for you. Everything will work out fine, Mma. I can feel it in my bones.'

'Your bones had better be feeling right,' you say, loosening yourself from his tight grip.

'My daughter lives in Wales!' the old lady says.

'Really?' Your eyes widen with excitement.

'Yes, she just bought a house in Wales and has invited me to come spend some time with her. You know how lonely it can get with one person in a big house. She lives at the very heart of Swansea,' she says.

You perk up at the mention of Swansea. 'God works in

mysterious ways, Mama. I have been looking for someone living close to the University. I have a friend in Wales but she lives in North Wales. She says the place is called Wrexham.'

'Oh no! That is too far. I will talk to my daughter about you. She will surely have a room to spare,' Mama says.

'I said I could feel it in my bones that this meeting was divinely arranged. Thank you so much Mama,' Uba says, bowing a little. Mama pats him on the back and asks him to stand upright. You feel a new hope springing forth within you. You almost scream, but you don't want to jinx it. You and the other travellers are still waiting to start leaving the weighing and check-in area to the next point of search.

Mama reassures you that her daughter will help you settle in properly. Uba counts his blessings and follows you to the boarding barricade. You happily grab Mama's hand luggage, easing her burden while luxuriating in the prospect of meeting her daughter, who owns a house. You thank God for your husband's faith and charitable spirit. You hug him one last time and whisper sweet things into his ears. He responds and promises his love for you. You kiss, deeply, not minding anyone. People are saying goodbyes of their own. Uba waits for you to cross the barricade and waves at you one last time as you go to immigration.

When the old lady moves swiftly and without the initial feeling of pain in her strides, you do not notice. When she hurries through her immigration checks and walks on, you are only too happy to grab your hand luggage and her small box. When the machine beeps and you are asked to declare the items in the box, you happily tell the immigration officers that it is an old woman's bundle of personal effects. The immigration officer lowers his glasses and gives you a withering stare.

'Oh no. I am not talking about myself. I meant the old lady you searched just now,' you say, still smiling.

'Open the bag,' the officer says, adjusting his glasses.

You fiddle with the zip, but there is a shiny padlock you did not notice before.

'Can someone help me call the old lady who just left the queue? She is with the key. I am just helping her with the bag,' you say.

By the time the immigration officers gather in their numbers and ask you to a corner for questioning, the old lady has speed-walked to the waiting flight. When they take you to their small room, break the padlock and unwrap the items in the small box, you keep looking around for the old lady, telling the immigration people that you are only helping a tired old woman who has just walked towards the boarding plane. When the officer going through the items brings out a smooth tuber of yam, you stare wide-eyed. *Yam in hand luggage?* When he pulls out a small knife from his drawer and slices through the tuber of yam to reveal a layer of white powder, you gasp. Your eyes well up as tears stream down your face. The other officers help themselves, slicing and cutting across a tube of toothpaste, a bar of soap, and an opaque water bottle. Everywhere, white powder.

'Where exactly did you say you were going, and for what purpose?'

'I am on a student visa to Swansea University, but I'm first going to Wrexham to stay in a friend's house 'til I get accommodation in Swansea,' you reply. You give much information so that the immigration people would believe you.

The officer stands and starts speaking in a clipped voice. 'Madam, you have the right to remain silent. You have a right to a lawyer. Anything you say can and will be used against you in a court of law.'

You watch, transfixed, as though outside yourself, as the officer snaps a pair of handcuffs around your wrists.

Now, you remember all the books you read about Wales to prepare for your journey. You read Dylan Thomas' works and River Tawe's history. You have dreamt of going to the Glynn Vivian Gallery as soon as you find a place in Swansea. You made several journeys to different places in Swansea through the pages of books and YouTube videos. You even picked up some Welsh words and used them around the house.

'Madam, please move. Don't let me rough handle you,' a female officer who has been quiet says, tapping you on your left shoulder. You shudder and turn to look the officer in the eye. It is then you realise that the immigration people with their tan uniforms have been joined by grey-wearing officers from the National Drug Law Enforcement Agency, NDLEA.

'You need to check the cameras; you will see the old woman.' You sound calm; you hope that they too will realise what is obvious to you, that they will at least check. You look around. 'There are cameras, right?'

'Just move, Madam.'

You suddenly realise that common sense will not prevail. You get desperate and try to struggle with the officers. You want to shout, make your point, be free to go to Wales and be a pathfinder for your family.

'Madam! Please respect yourself,' the first officer who asks you aside says. His voice is stern, his mien uncompromising.

Your dreams float in front of you and dissolve in a pool of tears. The scales of innocence fall from your eyes and shatter into reality. Your calmness dissolves as you suddenly realise your journey has taken a wrong turn. You try to get your phone to call your husband. One of the officers grabs it and pushes you. *'Move!'* You recall that Nigerianism that your people say when misfortune befalls somebody at the very edge of success. *His village people have got him.* You don't have the time or the presence of mind to think about these village people who are never there when anyone succeeds, who only show up to scuttle progress at the end of all longing. You start resisting and shouting.

'Oga. Oga, please. The bag is not mine. The old woman, the expensive looking one with the white lace, she... Check the cameras.'

'Move!' The officer says and they start pushing you.

You see a pool of water ahead as they lead you through the very route you had carried the hand luggage. On getting closer, you find a map of dirty dryness where the water once shimmered and shone.

As they lead you to a cell, a voice comes on the overhead speakers in the airport. 'This is the final boarding call for British Airways flight EZ9753 going to Heathrow...'

It is your flight.

Wild Romances

by Kate Waddon

The service station foyer was an unforgiving place for a family in meltdown.

'Mike, I'm just popping to the loo before we go.'

Billy was starting to make his faces. These usually led to visceral shouting with a bit of kicking thrown in. Amy, the oldest, scuffed her feet on the tiles in a bored tap dance. Three-year-old Nia was waving her arms wildly in her efforts to talk over everyone else, as if flapping could make her voice soar above the noise. Mike was frowning.

'Can't you take at least one of them with you? I mean, look at Billy, he's about to have a tantrum...'

'I'll be quick.'

'Mummymummymummy I seen a girl in a Hello Kitty T-shirt just like mine and she...'

'That's nice, honey,' was called over her shoulder as she half-ran to the Ladies'.

The coolness of the cavernous lavatories was weirdly comforting. She chose a cubicle at the far end and collapsed, exhausted, on the seat. Even by their family's usual chaotic standards, lunch had been hard work, and that was after 150 miles of refereeing the backseat battles...

She tried not to see Billy's behaviour as just plain annoying, but it was hard. Today's problems had been caused by his little sister touching him after eating a Chicken McNugget. Frazzled by the journey, frustrated as she'd watched her own meal collapse into cold sogginess, she had wanted to shout, "Oh for God's sake, a Chicken McNugget crumb is not going to hurt you!" but knew that this would be as provocative as it was pointless.

She was too tense to wee, and just sat there, her thoughts churning over her dismal lunch, then her dismal life. How had she not realised it would be like this? She didn't remember her childhood being like this, or seeing her Mam look anything more than mildly exasperated. The constant effort of being patient, the inability of his sisters or father to even scratch the surface of Billy's needs made her want to scream.

She hadn't even wanted three. Why had she given in? Must have been during one of those now-distant, mellow moods she used to have. Looking back over her past felt like remembering a film or a novel; detached, all about somebody else. Glazed with the relentlessness of it all, she half-read the advert on the back of the door. And read it again. And a third time. She couldn't face standing up, not yet. Billy would be building up to a shout by now. She was sure she could hear him over the thrum of the hand-dryers and the little-girl chatter. Giving up, she put the lid down and drew her feet up onto the seat. Foetal, she sat there. Invisible. She could stay here for ages.

A thought came.
How long would they take to notice if I didn't go back?

Could she stay here, in the ladies, for ages? Just to have a break? Keeping her feet up on the seat like in all the best thrillers? No. Mike would send Amy in to drag her back, and Amy, a completer-finisher if ever there was one, would shout under every door until her mother gave in and reappeared.

Maybe I just don't go back.

And like she was standing on a cliff edge, feeling that "what-if" impulse, she had the need to find out what would happen next.

Why should I go back?

What if I don't go back?

She stood up, suddenly awake.

I won't go back!

Action.

Decisively, she pulled her jumper over her head. Under it, she had a green vest top. A bit cold, but she was definitely not a woman in a black V-neck anymore. She stuffed the jumper in her tote bag. Now for the rest of her. They would be looking for a woman with long brown hair, so she pulled her hair into a twist then knotted it around itself. There. From a distance it could probably pass as short hair.

So, what to do first? She could go for a coffee. Hiding in plain sight and all that. Too risky. How about checking into the Travelodge at the end of the car park? Laying low until the initial search and panic blew over. She giggled to herself. It sounded like she was part of some criminal heist. But no. They'd be bound to ask the hotel receptionist if an under-dressed woman with no luggage had booked in.

She remembered seeing the sign for a shower earlier, next to the baby change room and just outside the lavatories. Billy had been most interested that a café should have such a thing. That was it.

She would hide in the shower room where Amy couldn't spot her, and then if her family left the lobby she could sneak out.

She went over her plan in her head. Hide in the shower room until the four of them moved away. Sneak out, find an ATM and get some cash. She'd need cash so they couldn't trace her cards: who said crime dramas weren't educational? Then what? Hitch a lift somewhere? Surely that was just asking for trouble, but were potential pervs and weirdos really interested in the likes of her, a forty-three-year-old, child-wrecked woman with ratty hair and a glazed expression? Ah, and carrying wodges of cash.

Leaving the toilet cubicle, checking around for signs of DCI Amy, she walked cautiously out of the Ladies' towards the lobby. Where were they? Nia was easy to spot. She was wearing an outfit of her own creation. Hello Kitty and Peppa Pig vied for attention across a background of eye-watering pink and orange. Billy was quieter now, but his mouth-stretching movements showed that the moment still hadn't passed.

They had moved along and were standing by the opener machine. She had no idea what these containers of plastic delight were really called; you put money in, wrestled with a twisty little knob and a cheap toy in a ball came out. As a child she'd named them "openers", and this had stuck. All three children were gazing at them. Mike was looking at his watch.

Moving quickly, she darted from the lavatory entrance to the shower room and shut the door. First mission accomplished. The shower room was small and dingy, although passably clean (possibly because the lighting was so dim but she didn't want to think about that). She couldn't imagine stripping off and showering at a service station.

So, cross to the services on the eastbound side of the motorway, get a taxi to the nearest town (definitely *not* hitching), then find a train to – where? Back home to Wales, of course. Where else could she possibly go, but home?

Then what? Her mind went blank. She'd think about that later.

For now, her thoughts were running through the practicalities of her everyday life, risk-assessing her absence. What about work? Well, there'd be plenty of other bored, middle-class ladies willing to step on each other's Boden pumps for a part-time job at the benign little C of E school, with its firm-but-fair headmistress and grumpy pet pig. Mike would be fine. He probably wouldn't even notice. Although he'd need to use Google Maps to do the school run. The children? She went blank again. She'd think about that later, too.

Unlocking the shower room door and opening it a crack, she peered out, and saw that the little group was still next to the opener machine. Why was Mike incapable of doing something entertaining with them, even for two minutes? Look at the leaflet rack or stare at the bright display outside Smiths or even buy them the sodding openers.

Mike was holding onto Billy's hand. Correction, his foot. Billy was on the floor, legs waving, face contorted (but at least he wasn't shouting). Amy was dancing around in circles, like she always did when she had to wait more than ten seconds for anything. Nia was gazing at the brightly-coloured little domes in the opener machine, hopefully. Mike looked at his watch again.

Come on, move. Go somewhere. They are still too close...

Then – ursus ex machina. A figure in a once-bright yellow bear costume lumbered towards the group from the direction of Costa. Nia immediately abandoned her opener scheme and skipped towards him. She didn't wait. While they were distracted, she sprang from the shower room, turned left and went straight out of the back door of the services into the lorry park.

Over the bridge. The other side of the services was nice, she noted with a strange sort of envy. Maybe if they'd been on this carriageway and gone to these nice services Billy wouldn't have had a meltdown and she and Mike wouldn't have snapped at each other and the girls wouldn't have bickered and she'd be back in the nice warm car instead of shivering in a vest top in November looking for an ATM and an escape route.

She found a cashpoint near (the nicer) Costa. No queue, excellent. As the machine spat out the notes, she felt almost giddy with bravery. Turning round, stuffing notes into her wallet, she took in the foyer of the busy services. There were people everywhere, mostly families caught up in the Sunday-afternoon, post-weekend-trip home journey. Clutching her wallet, she leant against the tiled wall by the ATM, watching. Nobody looked happy. Nobody looked like they wanted to be there, even on the nicer side of the carriageway.

An almost-forgotten line from *Mary Barton* came into her head: *How do you know the wild romances of their lives?* And how can you? And what was her wild romance? Boredom? Tiredness? The sick, grey feeling that every day was the same and would be forever and ever, the monotony broken only by tantrums and arguments? *Tomorrow and tomorrow and tomorrow...*

Her wild romance was not enough to ruin people's lives. The cliff face loomed in front of her again. Once more she felt that dizzy feeling that all it would take was one step and the monotony would be over.

The cliff receded. She stepped back.

Mike looked at his watch. Was there some sort of invisible string between his wrist and his face?

'What kept you?'

'Sorry. Dodgy tummy.'

Crouching down, she gently lifted Billy up by his hands, then she smiled brightly at the girls.

'Come on. Let's go to Smith's and get some magazines for the car.'

'Hooray!' Nia skipped ahead, energised by the thought of loot. The children took ages choosing. She flipped listlessly through a copy of *Hello*. Irrelevant images showing the glittery lifestyles of the rich and glamorous shimmered past her. More unknown wild romances, hidden under a layer of fame and foundation.

At last, the magazines were chosen, and the whole family clumped down to the till. Wearily, she noticed that Mike was peering into her purse. She had known he would, so she had an excuse ready. 'I've got to pay the ballet teacher tomorrow. She always asks for cash.'

He grunted; again, as she'd known he would. 'Bloody self-employed tax dodger.' But he accepted her reason, and she paid for the brightly coloured magazines with twenty pounds of her escape fund.

She glanced up at the clock above the counter. Almost half-past. The whole hide-and-escape thing had lasted barely twenty minutes.

'OK, come on kids, back to the car. Time to head home.'

Mike drove. She leant back against the headrest and dreamed about night trains on mountain passes.

The King of the Fairies

by Carolyn Thomas

Uncle Gildas lived in the Eye of the Sun (to give it its English translation). More importantly, Uncle Gildas had a shed. The door was kept locked, sometimes with an ancient bike, his transport to work at the brewery, propped against the door. Intrigued, we peered through the window to see inner tubes hanging like tired intestines, tins and bottles which we deemed to hold magic potions, strange glass vessels, including some I recognised as demijohns from my father's own experiments in wine making.

It was a cornucopia, a Tardis for the '50s. If anyone required anything, it would be produced or made – Uncle Gildas was always making things, although Uncle Steffan made the best wooden toys. The shed yielded all sorts of wonders: once, a birdcage for a disorientated budgie that found itself living wild in Uncle Steffan's garden. Captured, Joey seemed to dwell in darkness, his cage covered with a green velour cloth whenever we visited. Auntie Kitty, who showed an occasional blithe indifference to the truth, always explained 'Joey's asleep.' Only later did I discover that Joey's limited vocabulary was considered unfit for small ears when my cousin Michael revealed, in solemn tones, 'Joey swears.'

The gathering at Llygad yr Haul betokened another family crisis. When we arrived, the room was already thick with smoke from Gildas' 'Franklyn's Shag', rolled in impossibly thin cigarettes. My uncles and my Auntie Elen sat with funereal faces.

'Dai,' Gildas nodded at my father.

'Gil. No Non?'

By now, you will have recognised my grandmother's affectation for naming her offspring after Welsh saints, a tradition, thankfully, none of them were inclined to inflict on their own children.

My father's question was met with rolled eyes and Uncle Steffan's hacking cough. It was generally recognised that my aunt, Non, (irreverently dubbed by Michael, "Non of that nonsense," after her favourite scold) would wish to make an entrance, having a reputation for the dramatic, as well as the misanthropic. But before anyone could answer, tiny Auntie Mary whisked me into the kitchen, where she would remain for the duration, drinking tea and worrying.

'Mair's in the garden. Why don't you go out and play? But mind you don't go into the woods.'

It came as no surprise that, of my cousins, only Mair was present. On these occasions, those of us young enough to require supervision were farmed out between the aunts. I rushed out to greet her but, initially, she seemed to have vanished. I found her at the back of the shed, its door mysteriously open, with a paintbrush in her hand.

'Let's do something for Uncle Gildas.' She pointed to a tin of paint, its lid already prised open. I picked it up and followed her out.

'Stand back,' she instructed, taking stock of the canvas for her artistic efforts. Half an hour later, the east facing side of the shed, away from the house, bore the threatening message BEWAR, her sense of scale defeating my insistence it was missing a final letter.

'Girls.'

The King of the Fairies

Auntie Mary's voice came from the kitchen. Mair dropped the paintbrush and was about to join me in heading inside when I pointed to the tell-tale sign of paint on her hands.

'You go, Cerys.'

Auntie Mary smiled, 'I've made you some jam sandwiches so you can have a picnic, but mind you don't go into the woods.'

Few words, but they carried a clear instruction to stay out of the house and in the garden. There seemed little point in relaying them to Mair. She was a year older than me, and my hero. She was the best climber of us all, better than the boys, and nothing scared her.

'What did she want?'

I held out the bag of sandwiches. 'We can have a picnic.'

'Here?' The scorn in her voice was palpable. 'Let's go to the woods.'

I sighed at the inevitability of her response. It was true that Uncle Gildas' garden, with its neat rows of vegetables, had little to recommend it as a playground, and teasing his ferrets, pink-eyed and sharp-toothed in their cage, was not only forbidden but boring after a while. But the woods...?

Of course, I would follow her anywhere, adopting a show of courage I completely lacked, while looking anxiously backward to make sure Auntie Mary was out of sight.

I had been to the woods before, many times, but usually with my father or gentle Auntie Elen, who knew all about the trees and birds and told us stories about them: how birch bundles were used to drive out the spirits of the old year and the rowan tree, like the one in Uncle Steff's garden, kept witches away. Michael said, 'It doesn't work. Auntie Non still comes to our house.'

Auntie Elen looked reprovingly but failed to disguise the twinkle in her eye.

'That's unkind, Michael.'

'It's what Mam says.'

There could be no response since Auntie Kitty was well known for 'speaking her mind', perhaps a necessity when bringing up four unruly boys and Mair.

Those walks with Auntie Elen were a joy. She had no children of her own because she was *tragic*. Her fiancé had been killed in the war and she had never married anybody else which was a shame because she was still *beautiful*. The aunts (but not Non) said she was *dignified*, too. She didn't seem remotely tragic to us because she always had a lovely smile and laughed at our jokes. She delighted in indulging the rabble of nieces and nephews who clung to her like limpets. She told the most incredible stories, joined in our games, and, according to my mother, was *the voice of reason* whenever a crisis loomed.

The last time I'd been to the woods, there were no adults. It was twilight and there had been five of us, my older sister, Catrin, and my cousins taking turns to tell blood-curdling tales of witches, including Auntie Non, monsters and wicked fairies. I had a dangerously strong imagination and thoughts of that expedition raised a shudder as I followed Mair over the makeshift gate Uncle Gildas had erected between the spiteful barbs of holly that hedged the boundary between the garden and beyond.

Auntie Elen had said it was an Indian summer and the wood itself was benign that morning. The sun dappled the ground below the high beech trees, their leaves only hinting at a change of colour. There were still a few splashes of pink in the undergrowth where the red campion, *blodyn taranau*, the thunder flower, protects the fairies. They were the last of the blossoms, though: autumn was in the air.

The cluster of tiny scarlet berries on the cuckoo-pint was still glowing as we neared the dram road leading to the quarry. I was relieved when Mair crossed it because the quarry was treacherous. Long disused and flooded, with some rocks peering through the surface of the dark water like sharks' teeth, it was a sinister spot. Trees hung at crazy angles like comic skeletons between cracks in the craggy cliffs, and, Michael claimed, it was home to a monster that ate little girls. I didn't quite believe it but my father's words haunted me: 'If you fall in there, you won't come out alive.'

'Come on, slowcoach. We'll stop at the Fairy Glen.'

On this side of the track, the beeches gave way to lichen covered birches, rowan and oak. The blackberry flowers had shrivelled but the fruit, despite starting to change colour, were yet to ripen into the plump juiciness we greedily devoured or smeared over ourselves as war paint. As we made our way deeper into the wood, dangerous fungi, their bright colour a signal to warn off the unwary, were miniature versions of the one the Brownies danced around, or used to. Startling red with white spots, its cardboard was reduced to charred cinders when Mair and I, one enterprising Guy Fawkes night, decided to make it dance around us by placing a Jackie Jumper underneath it. Our career as Brownies was, predictably, short-lived.

Not far from the stream and past the Lion Rock, where I grazed my knee, showing off my climbing skills to an unimpressed Mair, the trees opened out and it was here we would have our picnic. As we approached, it was strangely quiet, apart from the woodpecker's monotonous drilling, and there, sitting on the fallen birch tree, was an old man we'd never seen before, a sketch pad in his hand.

He wasn't like Billy Twp, the tramp who came round a few times a year. Billy was dirty but *harmless* and, even in the summer, wore a scarf of Uncle Steffan's that Auntie Kitty had given him years ago, its colour indeterminate now. This old man didn't look like a tramp but was what my mother would have called *unkempt*, a term with which Mair and I were more than familiar.

He heard our approach, turned and looked directly at us.

'Well, well, young ladies. You must be Shenkin's granddaughters.'

I gasped and pulled at Mair's arm, dropping my bag at the same time so the sandwiches tumbled out. We'd always been told not to talk to strangers. Everyone in the village knew everyone else but we'd never seen him. We knew our grandfather only by name – he'd been a rollerman at the tinplate works and died when my father was still a child – so this was truly unnerving.

I reached for Mair's hand but she was bolder: 'How do you know us?'

The man winked and touched his nose with his index finger. 'I know everything.'

'Let's go,' I whispered, but Mair shrugged off my hand: 'Who are you?'

'I'm the King of the Fairies,' he said.

Mair's mouth dropped open.

'Don't you believe in fairies?' he smiled.

I found myself nodding and looked at Mair. She was nodding, too.

'Do you like to draw? I see you like to paint.' He pointed at Mair's hands and chuckled.

I was nervous about approaching him but Mair strode in his direction. 'Let's see what you're drawing.'

I found myself moving towards him to look at his sketch. It was a strange picture of the gnarled trunk of a birch tree.

'See them lines? That's the beetles' road, that is, and in that 'ole by there, there'll be baby birds next spring.'

I found myself looking closely at the picture and seemed to see it come alive with wildlife. It was like going for a walk with Auntie Elen.

'Do you want a sandwich?' Mair asked, casually confident.

He smiled. 'Even fairies have to eat.'

I'd forgotten about the sandwiches. I turned, bent down, and brushed off some soil. It was the sort of act that Auntie Non would have thundered at but he didn't seem to mind.

'Don't be frightened,' he said. 'I'd know that red hair anywhere. Are you Gildas' girls?'

'Steffan's,' said Mair and, emboldened, I said, 'I'm David's.'

'They was good boys. Gildas, too, and Elen, well... You love your Auntie Elen?'

We nodded furiously.

'Yes,' he said. 'Everybody loves Elen. Do she still 'ave red hair?'

I shook my head.

'Nah, it's white,' Mair replied. 'So's Auntie Non's, but she dyes hers black. Mam says she looks like a badger with her roots.'

He grinned. Perhaps he was aware that Auntie Kitty was less guarded in airing her opinions than she was about Joey's expletives.

He wasn't scary now. He knew our fathers and there was a softness in his voice when he said Auntie Elen's name.

Mair announced, 'Auntie Non is queen of the witches.'

We were startled by his loud explosion of laughter and so were the woodpigeons, their gentle coos replaced by the noisy sound of flapping wings as they soared indignantly from their perch. But he sobered quickly. 'There are no witches here, only wise women and good fairies. See the rowan trees? There are no bad witches where there are rowans.'

'Dad made rowan wine. It was horrible,' I found myself volunteering.

'Your grandmother used to make lovely wine.'

It was like a normal conversation. You could almost forget you were talking to fairy royalty. We munched on our sandwiches while he told us a story about Auntie Non and a bull until we cried with laughter. Then he said again, 'Do you like to draw?'

'I'm going to draw Auntie Non and the bull,' said Mair.

'Can I draw a fairy in the oak tree?' I asked.

'You can draw whatever you like. But can you see a fairy? The oak is the—'

'King of the trees,' we chorused.

'Very good. Now', he ripped pages from his book and presented them to us, with a stubby pencil for Mair and a charcoal stick for me, 'let's see what you can draw.'

All of sudden, it didn't feel right to draw a fairy. I looked at him and, as if he were reading my thoughts, he said, 'wait by 'ere and I'll show you something.'

He disappeared behind the big oak but soon returned holding something in his hands. He opened them to reveal a tiny ball of prickles.

I squealed with delight.

'Now then, here's something you can draw. But look quick so I can get 'im back before 'is Mam worries.'

I felt a pang of guilt. If Auntie Mary knew where we were, she'd worry, too, but it was fleeting and I settled down to try to capture the baby hedgehog on paper.

We sat quietly, finally producing our creations for him to look at. He smiled and praised our childish efforts.

'Can I keep these? And you shall 'ave one of mine.'

He handed me a rolled-up drawing. 'Don't open it 'til you get 'ome. And you should go now.'

I was astonished when Mair said, 'Thank you, your majesty,' and curtseyed, nudging me to do the same.

We walked back in silence. 'He didn't look much like a fairy,' said Mair.

'The tree didn't look much like the beetles' road,' I said, 'but it does now.'

She looked at me, surprised.

'Let's not tell.'

Auntie Mary, tired and frustrated after a morning of catering to bickering adults, failed to notice us climbing over the gate and we managed to escape detection when returning the paint to the shed, although I slipped, leaving a streak of white down my T-shirt. We hadn't realised quite how dishevelled we were until then: a small tear in Mair's shorts, the consequence of a brush with the holly as she scaled the gate; white paint still on her hands, charcoal stains on mine and both of us soiled from sitting on the ground. There really was no mistaking our delinquency.

'Look at them! Like navvies! *Ach y fi*! They've been in the woods!'

Auntie Non's shriek and apparent clairvoyance persuaded me she really was a witch.

Uncle Steffan grinned. 'Did you see any dragons?'

Ignoring him with a look that would have felled the most ferocious dragon, Auntie Non turned gimlet eyes on us.

'Let's have none of this nonsense, you naughty girls. Where have you been? The truth, now.'

My father, the mildest of men, interrupted.

'*Uffern dân*, Non. They're only a bit dirty!'

'And safe.' Auntie Elen's quiet words resounded.

'What's that you've got there, Cerys?' She held out her hand.

I had been hiding the King's present, still rolled up though a bit more creased, behind my back. Grudgingly, I passed it to her.

'And the paint!' Auntie Non was not to be silenced.

Uncle Gildas shot to his feet.

'*Arglwydd Mawr*! The shed!'

He rushed into the garden, closely followed by Auntie Non and by us. The legend BEWAR was all too evident. He dissolved into laughter before locking the door before any more damage could be done.

Back in the house, Auntie Elen had unrolled the King's drawing, a smile playing on her lips.

'What's that?' demanded Auntie Non.

'We met the...' Mair's glare interrupted me. 'We met an old man in the woods. He showed us...'

'Oh God,' gasped Auntie Mary, her hand flying to her mouth.

'A baby hedgehog,' I continued.

It was hard to answer when so many questions were being fired from different directions. The words 'talk to strangers' (don't), 'go in the woods on your own' (don't), 'disobedient', 'oh, God' (from Auntie Mary), 'badly brought up' (from Auntie Non), 'having fun' (from Uncle Steffan), spun around us. Only Auntie Elen said nothing.

With remarkable aplomb, Mair announced, 'It's OK. He knows you all. He told us about Auntie Non and the bull.'

I thought Uncle Steffan was about to die as he started to splutter and couldn't seem to stop. He was rocking back and forth, coughing, clutching his chest and convulsing with laughter.

'Oh, God,' Auntie Mary wailed.

To make her feel better, I told her he'd enjoyed her jam sandwiches, but that merely provoked an outburst from Auntie Non about cheeky brats.

Suddenly, everything went quiet as Auntie Elen said, 'Look at this drawing.' We all moved towards it. I'd faithfully kept my promise not to open it until we got back so I was as interested as everyone else, thinking, perhaps, there were more secrets like the beetles' road.

Looking back at me was a delicate portrait of Auntie Elen. But not as we knew Auntie Elen. Instead, it showed a young woman surrounded by birds. Nobody, not even Auntie Non, said a word.

Then my father said, 'The birds of Rhiannon have awoken your youth, Elen.'

Mair and I looked at each other, mystified. It sounded lovely but I had no idea what it meant.

'There's only one could have done that,' Uncle Gildas said quietly, 'and he's long—'

'Hush, Gil,' said Auntie Elen. 'Perhaps it's the magic of the woods.'

Unsurprisingly, it was Auntie Non who broke the comfortable silence. We were edging our way towards the back door when she caught us.

'Into the bath with you now!'

Auntie Mary looked worried, 'I don't know if there's enough hot water.'

'Serves them right. That'll teach them to do as they're told!'

'Oh, God!' Auntie Mary sounded exasperated and muttered something inaudible as we trudged upstairs behind her and waited while she filled the bath.

'Well, it's warmish so I suppose it'll have to do,' she said doubtfully.

Once she'd closed the door, we inspected the collection of pots and jars accumulated by our teenage cousins. Mair picked up one containing pink crystals, opened it and sniffed. 'What's this?'

'Bath salts,' I said knowledgably. Catrin had the same jar, a Christmas present from Auntie Mary, which she used sparingly while awaiting this year's contribution. Auntie Kitty had no time for such fripperies so it was a novelty to Mair who proceeded to empty the entire contents into the bath.

Up to our chins in bubbles, some of which were already overflowing and making their way onto the floor, we agreed. We'd never understand grown-ups. We didn't know, (and didn't care because it would have been boring), why the family had come together, and we couldn't understand why they all got so mysterious about the drawing of Auntie Elen. She was right about the magic of the woods, though: we had met the King of the Fairies, and it was our secret. But it was no secret that Auntie Non was a witch.

Summer's End

by Gosia Buzzanca

Today is the last day of the summer holidays and this just in – the princess is dead. I'm standing in the doorway of the living room in my nightshirt and I'm watching the news with my father. He's sitting in his chair, smoking sickly tobacco from a pipe, his legs crossed, the top one bobbing. The synthetic brown fabric of his seat is covered in craters melted out by the cigarettes that burnt through as he slouches, drunk, into sleep night after night. We don't know much about "the kingdom" here but looking at the two little princes makes me sad.

My mum is due to come home today.

For breakfast, I make myself sweet tea with lemon and a slice of sourdough bread with cream cheese. I eat and I browse magazines; pages full of Spice Girls and Leo DiCaprio, letters from the readers with words like erection and masturbation that make my skin prickle. I listen to *MMMBop* on repeat. Dancing, waiting, daydreaming about Taylor Hanson's hair.

My hair is chin-length now, the colour of cola. It fizzes in the light. I had it cut in May – it's a tradition for us girls to have our hair chopped after the First Holy Communion – and my shoulder-length plaits went down in two quick slashes at the hairdresser. Another thing we do is buy white leather clogs, the soles of them so heavy – we can't walk in them properly, so we slump and drag our feet all over the place instead. I feel so mature now that I know the taste of the Lord's body.

'Kasia!' I can finally hear my friend's voice. 'Ka-sia!'

'Coming,' I lean out of the window, put a hand on my throat, cross my eyes, and point a finger to my door, then press it to my lips – I seal it, lock it, and throw her the key.

I make my father a coffee. Turkish style with two sugars, no milk. I place the steaming glass next to the remote control. I've watched mum do it. Most of the time we're a quiet household.

'I'm going out with Lena,' are the first words I say to my father this morning.

So far this is a summer like any other. We've spent it telling ourselves stories about the ghost of a nun, digging about in the barren ground, playing twenty questions and hopscotch. A few days ago, I stole one of my father's cigarettes and Lena and I hid behind the block and took turns smoking it. We choked and the smoke tasted like an ashtray, so I picked up eight green apples that had fallen from our tree before their time. We ate them all and not long after that I had to run behind the block again, this time to be sick all over my hands like I wanted to catch it or something. The smell and taste of the smoke were gone then.

As we walk towards the bushes Lena bursts out laughing.

'Remember the tape?' she asks.

Yesterday Lena brought out her Walkman and a tape that had a recording of her parents doing it. She's two years older than me and so brave. Like most of our flats, the living room doubles up as her parents' bedroom, and she sneaked into there, pressed record on the Hi-Fi. We took turns at the headphones and giggled ourselves to tears.

'What time is your ma back today?' Lena picks a handful of yellow egg plums from the bush and shoves them all in her gob at once, then picks some more and passes them to me.

'Soon, I guess.'

Both our mums are poorly this year. Hers spent two weeks in the hospital at the end of June and mine, due to complications, has been away for the whole of August. Lena's mum had all her lady bits cut out and can't have more children. Not that she wanted them, but it's nice to have options, I suppose.

My mum is away with kidney stones. They run in our family.

We're spitting out the fruit pips as we walk into the bushes. They've been our base for three years now, and every spring, as soon as it's dry and warm enough to ditch coats, all the kids that live in the block step over the brambles and wild things that managed to appear over the cold months. We're reminding nature who is in charge here.

My skin feels sticky as I climb my tree. We each have a tree that we are married to, and we can spend hours like this – necking the bark, licking its irregularities, smoothing our husband's faces with tongues. We have our trees polished, luminous, shiny. Well-loved.

'Enough for me,' says Lena.

'What?' I reply, wiping my mouth.

'This... game.'

I can feel the red rising in my cheeks. The only time I felt good this summer was when I was holding a tree trunk in my hands, whispering sweet nothings into it.

'Anyway,' Lena continues, 'I got my period.'

A silence. My mouth makes a big "O". Only the other week I'd stuffed my knickers with mum's sanitary towel. I did it the wrong way around by mistake. The glue stuck to my body, and I bled after all, trying to remove it. I told nobody.

'So now I need to find a real boyfriend. You see how being married to the trees is a childish game, right?'

That word again. The tears come and make my eyes feel sharp as if there are bits of sand under my eyelids. My fingers work away at a loose piece of bark.

'She's here,' says Lena.

'Who?'

My chest jumps. I know the answer.

I follow Lena's eyes and from between the leaves, I can see my mum. She's being led towards our block with the help of a nurse. Father is two steps behind them, carrying the bags. The dress she wore a month ago hangs off her now. Her skin looks paler than usual, and her ginger hair seems frizzy, the way it does before a proper blow-dry. I want to run to her but at the same time, I don't want Lena to see us. I'm embarrassed by the way I love her.

'Anyway, do you know what she was in the hospital for?' Lena asks.

'Duh, the kidneys.'

'Nope. What she was in there for, *for real*,' she smirks. 'Same as mine.'

She laughs now and pretends her fingers are scissors.

'She'll be fucked for weeks.'

Lena jumps off the tree and makes her way out of the bushes.

'See you after lunch?' she tosses over her shoulder.

I watch her until she disappears and then I kiss my tree. I'm deliberate with it: gentle lips first, then licks of the tip, then full tongue, deep into the cracks, until I feel the tiniest of cuts form. My saliva tastes like metal and wood.

The misery of missing my mother felt like a hole in my belly all month, but now she is back and instead of patching itself, the hole fills up with sick.

Lunch is a sandwich with cheese and tomatoes sprinkled with chopped onions, salt and pepper. I usually slurp the remaining tomato juice from the dish but I'm not in the mood today. The food is dry. Chewy.

Father has turned the sofa into a bed for mummy. She's lying there with her bones like a bunch of sticks poking through her grey skin. I try to think that she's pathetic but really, I just feel sad. The telly is still on from the morning, now a parade of speakers mixed up with flashy shots of the princess in her dresses, her jewels, her blue eyeliner.

'What were you up to, sweets?' mother asks.

'You know. Playing with Lena. Trying to grow things on our plot.'

'I've missed you,' her eyes are reaching out to me, but I shrug, and she retreats. I can feel my eyes starting to sting again. I run out of the room.

The afternoon crowd is bigger. The morning mass finished, the chicken soup consumed, the Sunday Best removed. All the kids are out for the last afternoon of freedom.

There's seven of us in total. Three girls, four boys. One thing we have in common, other than living in the same block, is that at least one of our parents is a teacher. The holiday means more for us – we don't get any other break from school. We have to be on our best behaviour all the time.

Lipstick Eyebrows

'Why did you miss the church?' asks Alex.

He's my age but the size of a pre-schooler. Last summer we played doctors in the playground and I still can't get over what I saw in his pants. No matter the shock, I lay inside the dirty tunnel and spread my knees wide. He ran away like it was about to bite him.

'I keep telling you.' The kid sure is slow. 'I never go when my mum is away. Nobody makes me.'

My dad believes in God but not in church as an institution, that's what I heard him say once. Now that mum is back, she'll take me to the confession as soon as she can. Hopefully.

Lena still hasn't said a word to me. I hope she feels bad about earlier.

'What should we do then?' one of the boys asks.

I definitely want to do something; I'm still sad. I stopped feeding my Tamagotchi and it's done two poos now that I didn't clean. Sometimes I want to see how quickly it could die, but I always react before it's too late.

'Should we go jump in the hay?' I offer.

Lena raises her eyebrow, and the others start talking between themselves.

At the edge of our town, in a field, there's haystack storage owned by the Russian guy everyone always gossips about because he has a funny accent. The hay is for the horses on his farm and is protected by a tin roof and three concrete walls. I see it every time we go to the supermarket.

'Sounds perfect,' Lena makes it sound like it was her idea. 'Let's move it!'

We make our way across the town. It's humid, barely a breeze. We march through the air that smells like chocolate pudding, the way it always does this time of year when the waffle factory overheats.

'Good afternoon!' we sing in unison to every person that passes by. We get in trouble if we don't.

We storm alongside the main street – only a grocery store, a bookshop, a second-hand clothes place and a post office. Ala, the third girl, holds us back behind the guys and unzips her bum bag, showing us a can of beer.

'We really shouldn't,' I say.

I think alcohol is scary because I know it's the reason my parents shout at each other, but they look at me like they would at a baby.

'Fine,' I give in.

We duck behind the red-brick train station and take turns of three sips each. The beer is the lemon kind. It's surprisingly sweet. The speed at which we drink gives us a buzz. By the time we catch up with the boys, we can't stop laughing.

The hay scrapes our knees that are already covered in bites and bruises. It wriggles inside our socks like insects. We brush it off and carry on as we were, deranged with joy, piling stacks on top of each other and screaming loud as we jump down.

'Freedom!'

'Holidays forever!'

We know we shouldn't be here, but we gain more courage by the minute. One of the boys lights up a cigarette and passes it around. Lena smiles at me. I wince.

'Should we get a fire going?' suggests Alex.

'You're so fucking dumb,' someone replies.

'Never play with a fire or you'll wet yourself at night,' I say because it's what my mum told me; there's a pang in my tummy and I miss her again.

We start to chase each other instead. There's so much hay. I throw handfuls of it at whoever is running behind me. It feels like a music video – straw everywhere and the dust is rising from underneath our feet. It makes us cough, sticks to our skin.

'Hey,' Lena catches my wrist and pulls me away from them now.

'What?' I growl. 'What do you want?'

'Shhh,' she says. 'Come.'

She leads me to the edge of the storage, into a labyrinth of haystacks. It looks like a den. On the ground there's a bunch of cigarette ends and a torchlight, some scrunched up paper. A manky blanket in the corner.

It's surprising how familiar she seems with the place. I'm still breathless and angry, but something in me releases.

'I come here on my own sometimes,' she admits. 'Some nights I get out of the flat through the balcony and come here to read and smoke.'

My mouth drops – it's a hell of a trek to do on your own, especially in the darkness. But this is Lena, after all. If she can slide in on her parents having sex, she can slide away unnoticed too.

'I'm sorry about earlier,' she says. 'The princess thing got to me, and I was just so angry at them for being ill on us like that.'

I nod.

'Anyway, I hoped you may wanna try something new,' she looks about as if to spot anyone coming. 'With me.'

She's next to my face. Her eyes are closed. I hold the air in. She undoes the button of my shorts. Slips her hand inside. It tickles. Her lips are on mine now. She's trying to force her tongue inside. My teeth are shut. I shiver.

'I knew you would like it.'

She's pulling my shorts down. My bunny underwear. She licks

the top of my legs. She licks my belly button. She licks her finger and stuffs it inside me. I wish it would bite her.

'Please stop.'

She doesn't. I miss my tree. I slam my eyes shut and go somewhere else.

When I come back, I see a white cat running out of the labyrinth but other than that, I'm on my own.

'Kasia! Ka-sia!' a whisper that's both angry and scared comes out of nowhere.

I'm surrounded by haystacks. My shorts are around my ankles; my legs are shaking and I'm so thirsty.

'Kasia!' It's Alex, I see him gaping from above.

I must look a right mess.

'What are you doing there?' he asks and in the same beat adds, 'Quick, a car is coming.'

The Russian. I pull up my trousers, but my hands are shaking now too, and I fumble with the button. My heart is in my throat, trying to escape, just like I'm struggling to make my way out of here. I can't find my shoes.

I decide to climb up to where Alex was standing just a moment ago. The hay cuts my feet. When I reach the top, I can see him running out of the storage unit. He keeps turning to see if I'm behind. Ahead of him, already on the road, the rest of the crew.

Everything slows down. I can hear the screech of the tires. The engine stops. The door opens – loud disco music – and shuts. A few steps and a horrible scream.

'Fucking, shitting hell!'

The Russian runs in circles assessing the damage. His hands move from his head to his hips like he can't believe his eyes.

'Hello?' it comes out of me like a mouse squeak.

I do the sign of the cross and that's when he looks up.

A pair of dry hands grab my bare ankles and pull me down. I can feel a volcano erupting in my stomach: embarrassment spreads under my skin to my toes, the tips of my fingers. My face is burning.

'I knows you,' says the Russian.

Everyone knows everyone here.

'I... I'm very sorry.'

His head is shaved and there is a crescent scar across his brow bone. His eyes are green and scaring me. We were trespassing. I've been caught – as always, the slowest.

He considers me, eyes rolling over my unbuttoned shorts, the loose straw stuck to my chest, my sweaty cheeks. I look at my bare feet.

'How many of you was 'ere?' he's asking.

'Six. Seven.' I have forgotten myself.

The Russian is nodding now, must be surprised at the ease with which grassing up came to me. He takes a notebook from the back pocket of his jeans and a pen from his shirt.

'I want names, and addresses.'

I give him everything I can.

'Lil' motherfuckers, you lot,' he says.

I lower my head. His eyes seem unfocused now as if covered in cling film.

'Turn around,' he demands. I don't, so he forces my torso to, throwing me at the haystack and grabbing at my wrists behind my back. He's squeezing hard, pressing his thumb into the cushion of my hand. I can smell sweat, danger and alcohol.

'Imma call the pigs on you lot next time,' he whispers. 'Go.'

He releases me. I trip. There's not enough time to look for my clogs. I get up and run out of there, into the field, then onto the road.

The sun is on its way down, turning the sky into a blue and pink watercolour; the rain must have fallen nearby. I can smell it. My heels are sinking into the still-hot asphalt, leaving tracks as a wild animal would. Insects stick to my face.

Everything is quiet outside the block. No kids. Are they hiding at home, waiting for their trouble? I hope so.

The neighbour takes her washing off the line.

'The wind is picking up!' she spots me.

'Aye, going to rain soon.'

'Say hello to your ma, will you?' I nod. 'Hope she heals quick and that.'

The coolness of my staircase brings relief. I lean my forehead against the brown, oil-painted wall. I practice my happy face before I go inside.

The kitchen is filled with a golden light, the way that only happens on these summer evenings. There's a big pot on the stove full of still-warm tomato soup; its familiar smell like a hug. I drink three tall glasses of water. The thick curtains are drawn close in the living room, the telly is still on but muted. Mum's monstera plant casts a shadow on the old wallpaper. I tiptoe to my bedroom. My uniform hangs from the wardrobe door – black skirt, the white blouse. She somehow managed to get it ready for me. Everything is pressed and clean, thick with its newness. On the chair, still in its packaging, is a fresh pair of tan tights – no bare legs allowed – and underwear. My shoes are polished, too.

In the bathroom, I have a quick shower and pop a new pair of pyjamas on. The rest of the clothes I wore I bury – my shorts, my bunny pants, my top – at the bottom of the wash basket. I brush my hair, teeth – twice. Smudge some Nivea cream on my cheeks – the smell of it reminds me of my grandma.

Mummy is asleep on her sofa-bed. Father's chair is empty. I hold my breath and I slip under her blanket. I rest my head in her armpit, careful not to wake her. I put my arm around her, mindful of the wounds. She's warm. I grab her hand and count her fingers.

'One, two, three...'

She told me that when I was a baby, she would count my fingers and toes each morning and every night, making sure they were complete. Hers are now.

She wakes, confused. Tries to stretch out but I sense that it's painful. Her face is smiling even though her eyes tell a different story. Mummy squeezes me lightly.

'Are you excited about school tomorrow?'

Lipstick Eyebrows

by Naomi Paulus

The Call
Little Ears calls the house phone at 2am and Mum answers it. I already know, even in my in-between-sentience in between the sheets, because there is only one reason the house phone would ring now. It is the night manager. Two days after the summer solstice so the darkness is short. She will die tonight. Then we will go back to bed.

    Mum stands in the hall and relays the information while I lay in my childhood bedroom next to a grown man, my boyfriend. When I reach for my bedside lamp a salmon pink glow spreads across the room, like a torch shining into a womb. It's the colour of closed eyelids when they can't hold back the sun. I can't tell if my eyes are open or closed because either way all I see is hot retinal pink. Bloody pink. Decades ago, Dad had said my wall paint selection might be too bright but he believes in only giving his opinion and then letting his children make their own mistakes. Always one shade lighter than you think you want girls. Sadness is often described as grey, like a dark fog or a black dog, but really it is this mauve desaturated colour trapped behind your eyes. It's the peach bathroom suite in your grandmother's house with matching fluffy covers around the toilet seat that look cosy but are saturated in piss. Disarmingly joyful in its horror.

Getting up, eyes now open but unfocused, I push my arms through the curled-up sleeves of a cardigan and even though the clothes come crumpled from 'the chair', I don't sniff them first. I hear my boyfriend ask if he should come and I say no, there's no need, while I turn off the bedroom light and because he is English, he doesn't. I go to pee even though I'm not sure I need to and while I'm in there I grab a nail varnish from the bathroom cabinet.

As I walk down the stairs, someone else's life flashes briefly before me. It is hers. A woman who I understand only in relation to myself, who does not exist at any other age in any other timeline I can imagine. A member of the support cast who makes special appearances at birthdays. I can't shape it into an entire life, beautifully arced and meaningful, because I only have fragments from the end of it. I shake them out of my head.

In the hall, I go to pick up any pair of shoes that might fit and my sister enters from the kitchen. She is wearing her glasses too.

They have already left, she tells me without looking at me, referring to our parents. They do not want to miss the main event, the one we've all been waiting for, for weeks now.

While my sister searches for a pair of shoes that might fit her feet, settling on Mum's sandals, I tell her that Nan won't be impressed by our outfits –we haven't made enough effort. She doesn't even try to smile.

I think about the day when we arrived at the front door of Nan's seaside stone cottage, that used to be a pub on the Mumbles Mile, to find she had drawn on her eyebrows in bright 'Oral Tease' coloured lipstick. After the initial shock, I decided that the red streaks did at least fulfil their purpose of distracting from the line that stretched across her forehead. The scar from when they peeled back her head in the 80s. In fact, they even complimented her newly box-red hair scrunched up in a bun on top. (She only saw the brunette 'before' photo on the dye packet.) I told her what she had done but she just laughed and I couldn't tell if she already knew or not. Whether, maybe, the lipstick eyebrows were deliberate. She tilted her head back and laughed unselfconsciously loudly. Then she tried to push the laughter onto me by shoving my chest with her hard fingers.

I resist the urge to shove my sister now as she reaches for the car keys first in a blatant power-play. It is not the time to fight and she doesn't seem in the mood to laugh. Outside, the midsummer's night is still glorious and it makes me want to pause and admire the stars. The air, still dancing in heat from her last day, wraps its warmth around me so I don't need the cardigan after all.

I sit side by side with my sister in the front seats of the car, breathing deeply but not speaking. She takes a short steadying pause at the end of the drive. This is the third time we have received this call and driven through the night to a nursing home on the other side of Swansea. Third time lucky, I think and smirk to myself. My sister glances at me, noticing the change in my breath and I feel bad for making a joke on the way to our grandmother's deathbed. Even if it was only inside my head. I tell myself that this could be just like all the other times Little Ears called and we made this journey. It doesn't help much because death cannot really be avoided. And death, like sex, isn't like it is in the movies. For one thing, there has been much more foreplay.

The Drive

The drive from Sketty to the nursing home at the end of Rhossili begins sweeping around the curve of Swansea Bay and goes on to span the full length of the Gower, right to the very tip. As I look out from the car's passenger window, the landscape is stratified in thick dark lines. Road, sand, sea, rock, sky. Ever changing under the power of the waves that move the land, swelling and retreating. Looking across to Mumbles I can see the lighthouse turning its slow warning.

We are driving to be in the room when her body stops but a person dies in three distinct stages. Particularly if you are lucky enough to die this slowly. We began dismantling her life when we emptied her cottage to move her into the nursing home. Her material manifestation was built by small china trinkets and decorative occasional bowls. It gave the two-down of her home the atmosphere of a charity shop stock room, which, in a way, is exactly what it was.

Which way shall I go? My sister cuts through my thoughts.

Huh?

What's the fastest route? Can you look it up? She reaches across the divide between us to turn the radio on. My gaze is brought down to focus and fumble with my phone to confirm the route but she doesn't respond. I turn the radio up louder as she changes lane and the dial jerks upwards in my hand. After a second of deafening noise, I find the right volume level. Background music set, I focus on the road ahead, on the white dashes marking our progress along Oystermouth Road. The adverts come on and my brain still obligingly sings along to jingles for second hand cars.

The Mayals road takes us up to an open common where shaggy ponies haven't needed to shelter in the summer warmth and the speed limit increases. From here, passing over into the Gower, is an endless series of merging villages until we reach the end of the land. Murton, Bishopston, Kittle, Pennard. Each with its own history and folklore, new estates and primary schools. Sometimes, when people ask where I'm from because they can't tell from the accent I've lost, I say 'The Gower' instead of Swansea.

We cruise into Parkmill through the tall trees and old stones alongside Ilston stream. We pass the village shop, Shepherds, and next to it is The Gower Heritage Centre where my sister had her 8th birthday party. In addition to parties, the heritage centre was the destination of countless school trips, but I can't really remember it. I think it has terrible life-size figurines of olden-time people in Welsh costumes. It's stupid really because you can't teach a twelve-year-old about heritage. They have no point of reference. They're not calibrated properly yet.

My sister deftly winds between the hedges, an expert on country roads, and I see glimpses of the sea over the fields in the dark. I have the sensation of being moved. Flowing down a lazy river on a donut inflatable, relaxed but unable to move out of the stream. No option but to see it through to the end. You can freely make your only choice, I remind myself.

I couldn't have driven.

It isn't safe to be in control of a vehicle when you're so focused on your own journey that you completely forget that other people are on the road making their own journeys; with their own destinations in mind.

My phone lights up the car with a text from Dad.
Are you on your way?
I reply.
Yes. 20 minutes.

I check my watch. 2:30 AM. Our parents will have just arrived. I picture the scene: the carers, the bed, the breathing, the waiting and I have the sudden urge to turn back. To take control, grab the wheel, pull up the handbrake. Anything to show I still have self-determination. Just as the feeling becomes too much my sister swerves sharply, stops in the centre of the road and flicks on the full beam.

The heat from the engine swirls with the heat in the air in front of the headlights. We stare at the now well-lit creature in the middle of the road. A stupid dirty sheep. Typical. Lost, even though it bears the fluorescent markings of ownership on its flank. An external identity printed on for all to see and it's so dumb it still can't find its way back. Moron. For a moment, I wonder whether I brought this road block into existence through sheer force of will, until I notice my sister's hands are shaking.

The Wait
We park the car on the gravel outside the home, where the grass rolls into sand into rock into a sheer cliff face that drops into the sea. I can't stop myself from walking towards the edge and peering out into the abyss for comfort. It's a bit like looking into an empty bottle of wine. The same feeling of calm.

I hear my sister press the buzzer to the front door.

I kick the gravel half-heartedly.

Little Ears lets us in. I look at her cropped blonde hair as she makes professional sympathetic noises and I think, Nan is right, she does have really small ears. My sister is nodding at her and they take it in turns to make gentle affirmations back and forth while the other is talking. A verbal ceremony as Little Ears prepares us both to enter the sacred room. She walks us down the corridor and I resist running my hand along the wall bannister while taking a deep inhale – it smells of old-gravy-dried-into-hand-knitted-jumpers. Old people forget to wash their hands, I remind myself, and they soil themselves frequently.

Outside the room, Little Ears stops to knock and turns to watch us while she rests her hand on the doorknob. My sister continues with eye-contact pleasantries whilst I opt out to stare at the smiling picture of Nan they've stuck to her door. Maybe it's to remember whose room is whose, maybe it's to inspire a collegiate boarding school vibe, or maybe it's to serve as a reminder that real people existed before the decline.

Little Ears must hear consent from within because she opens the door and nods at us. Show time. I hang back, managing to stay a few more seconds outside the room, before following my sister in.

The room is hot and the air is heavy. Our grandmother's lungs labour under it. A fan spins in the corner, pushing air towards her, trying to force it down her throat. Mum is sitting close, holding Nan's hand tenderly but with two outstretched fingers, she's taking her pulse. I watch her lips count as she follows her wristwatch. My parents, who are the real adults and themselves doctors, are in charge now. I try to relax. Taking a seat behind my mother, I feel the nail varnish in my pocket and remember. I pull it out and show my sister.

We can't bury her with nails like that, I say. I want to add something like 'she'll be turning in her grave' but I need to sense the mood first.

My sister nods and heads to the ensuite, which is too fancy a word to describe an entirely waterproof room. We take over the vigil from Mum, who needs some persuasion to go with Dad to get a coffee in the staff's break room.

I take the warm, wet flannel from my sister and, turning back to

Nan, I dab at her thin skin to clean her hands. She gives them to me like a tired puppy might give a paw. Trusting and powerless. I drag the cooling cloth across her palms and down to each fingertip. I didn't bring a nail file so she's going down with claws. I massage in the hand cream I bought her for Christmas, turning over her palms to feel every swollen bone. On top of the existing chipped purple, I paint the Revlon Cadillac Red and it looks beautiful. As I hold her hands in mine, I notice the contrast between hers, all knuckles and nails, and my thin bitten stubs underneath. Both are grotesque in their own way. Her application of feminine conformity pushes so far past the realms of acceptability it becomes a perverse act of defiance in itself.

My sister brushes Nan's hair, teasing out her fringe to pull it down over her forehead, trying to cover the dent. I consider drawing on her eyebrows but the image is too macabre. Still, it might make Mum laugh when she comes back. An option if things get out of hand, maybe. Or perhaps just a note for the funeral director.

By now it is 3am, when time stretches out and the extra hours hide. The in-between-time. The in-a-minute-nows. Like the time between Christmas and New Year, the endless last week of August in Year 8, or an overnight flight to the other side of the world. The last thirty years of Nan's life have been extra time. Thirty years since the doctors removed a small amount of her brain and gave her six months to enjoy the rest. They short circuited her, released her from reality and made her happy. She spent the next decades content. On her daily shopping trips to town, she would go to the McDonalds in Castle Gardens for a coffee and a rest, enjoying the simple pleasures of cosmopolitan sophistication that Swansea had to offer.

While the nail varnish dries, I sit at her side. Her heart moving fast under the thin skin stretched across her ribs. I keep watching because there is nothing else to do, waiting patiently each time for her chest to rise again.

I shunt my chair in closer and take her hand.

My sister announces that she needs some fresh air and leaves me alone.

I'm here, Nan. I'm here.

With nothing else to focus on, I feel my breath start to falter with hers, stalling on the refill. I try to steady my breathing, exaggerating it to give her a strong rhythm to follow. Her mechanical inflating is somehow more powerful, cranked now by a primal force, and I fall in sync with her again.

By the time my parents return, I think I could be hyperventilating from the restricted holding pattern my ribs have been trapped in. I start gasping when I see my mother.

Her breathing has changed, the gaps seem bigger—

Mum waits a second.

No, she says and takes a seat, you will know when it changes.

Mum uses a small sponge on a stick to wet Nan's lips and tries to get her to suck on it. She won't. Other items at her disposal include a carton of protein milkshake with an opaque white straw jutting out. Mum picks the carton up to inspect it and to decide whether it is worth administering. After reviewing the back of it she declares it to be out of date.

I should tell them, they will want to know, she says, getting up to press the button to call a member of staff.

Dad says not to bother, they are understaffed and doing their best. He stops mid-sentence and I know it's because the rest of the sentence is that it's not going to kill her. I agree, she's almost expired herself. Propped up on pillows, stuck awkwardly to one side, her thin frame is sinking into the mattress. All her remaining energy has retreated deep within her body, just keeping the essential functions going, slowly accepting defeat as they surrender more ground.

The second stage of her death, after we disposed of her material possessions, was when her mind finally gave up the ghost in the machine. That is, the long chain of consciousness that she relied on for self-permanence broke. Formative experiences lost, she could no longer rely on the memory of her identity, on the self-assurance of actions and feelings building together over time to form her character. Shattered, she became a series of one-off responses to stimuli which, with nothing to link them, added up to nothing.

Of course, Nan's chain of consciousness had broken before, half way through her life. I didn't know her before the brain operation. The frontal lobe, to a certain degree, controls your personality. A lobotomy, or damage to this area can affect your emotions and reduce your inhibitions, as well as problem solving, memory and judgement. Nan certainly had no inhibitions; inside her head she was completely free from other people's judgement.

Hearing is one of the last things to fade, Dad says while turning on the CD player and I begin to regret openly talking about her burial in front of her. My sister comes back from her trip outside and claims that a group of teenagers are having a rave down on the beach. They have disco lights and everything. I lean my head out of the window and I can just about hear the muffled beat. Then Dad clicks play and the movement of air in the room changes. Like someone has turned off the taps.

She's breathing with her stomach and auxiliary muscles now, Mum explains.

Nan lurches forward in a convulsion and Mum catches her, cwtches her.

I know, Mam. I know.

Dad presses the buzzer to call Little Ears.

It is time for pain relief.

It was an aneurism the size of an orange that marked the transition from Nan's first self into her second. It is always the size of fruit. A squidgy tangerine inside her skull pressing on her optic nerve ready to explode.

There is a line dividing two halves of my life too and, although it doesn't physically stretch across my forehead, it has left a mark. My life was split when I left Wales at eighteen. Her, two different people in the same place. Me, the same person in two different places. I wonder what it would be like if I didn't feel the constant push and pull, the coming in and going out. Powered not by the moon like the tides but by First Great Western Rail and less reliable. Recently, I have started to doubt the truth I've known since childhood: that life is happening somewhere else but it is too late.

My accent changed after a professor told me at matriculation dinner that Welsh rarebit was a joke about how vulgar the Welsh are. Because it sounds like 'rabbit' which is the cheapest meat, not 'rare' at all, and the bloody Welsh can't even afford that so it's just cheese on toast. Then he told me which cutlery to use first. Now I can't get my voice back, no matter how much I want be that stupid little Welsh girl again.

The CD starts to skip on an orchestral rendition of Engelbert Humperdinck's 'Spanish Eyes'. Dad has to eject the disc to stop it and Little Ears arrives.

Lipstick Eyebrows

I need to call the out-of-hours GP to administer diamorphine because we can't keep it onsite, she explains.

Mum nods and asks who is on call tonight.

Dr Bevan.

Mum and Dad exchange a look.

Little Ears goes into the corridor to call him but we hear the exchange. She explains the situation, several times, no it can't wait until morning.

Please.

Dad gets up silently, walks over to the corridor and closes the door behind him. Mum exhales loudly and slowly, like she's hoping she can force whatever she's feeling out.

Nan, because it was her husband who died six months after the operation, not her, spent most of her time with us. She loved to swim in the sea on trips to the beach. Even though she only ever did a slow breaststroke with a full face and earrings still on, head staying motionless above the surface like a swan in drag.

Iesu Mawr, she would shriek as she waded into the cold water. Warning us to stay away from the jellyfish and their stinging testicles.

'Tentacles,' Mum would correct her and Nan would laugh but I didn't get the feeling she understood why. She laughed simply because she loved to laugh. Even when it was a completely inappropriate reaction, she would laugh. Laugh because someone was ill, laugh because she made a mistake, laugh because there was nothing else to do.

Then Mum leans in and reaches forward. She was right, even I can tell that there has been a change in breathing this time. Deflated and running out of air, her system is finally winding down. I move closer and take the hand that walked me home from school one more time. She gently squeezes me and I can't tell if she knows I'm there or not, whether it was on purpose or not.

The last of her reflexes are firing, like a line of small airbags jerkily inflating one by one in an automatic brace for impact. Then a long pause before the restart. Until the pause lasts and Mum checks her watch. 4.08 am. Something the size of a satsuma catches in my throat and I have to gulp it down.

A feeling starts to spread through my veins that I don't want to associate with my grandmother. I can't let it colour my memories. It is the same feeling as when the teenagers in McDonalds put ketchup and salt in her coffee. How they laughed at her and she probably laughed too. To me, she always looked so glamorous with her dyed hair and bright makeup. It was sometimes jarring to realise other people could see her at all, that she didn't just exist for me, and worse to think that they didn't see her the way I did. Her memory can be finalised now with none of that included. I package it up neatly and close my eyes to focus on her image, the one on the door.

The third and final stage, the physical shut down, is complete but I can't look away after spending so long fixated on the rise and fall of her bony ribs. They still look like they are paused on the cusp of re-inflation.

The carers come in and say goodbye. They call Nan a character. Hell of a girl. Wild, she was. They will miss her. I believe them. She was insane but it was in a fun way. In a truly alive way.

Then they leave us alone with the whirring sound of the electric fan.

After half an hour, Little Ears comes in and gently nudges to call the funeral home. They'll leave the fan on but it is very hot tonight.

Scab

by Ellen Davies

Turning into the terraced street, Caryl slammed on the brakes. In the middle of the road, a small boy stared at her from his trike. He was shoeless and clutching a sticky lolly in his left hand.

'Jesus,' Caryl muttered under her breath, then winding down her window, she called, 'get out of the road!'

The boy shuffled towards the pavement, his feet pushing the trike along. Caryl manoeuvred the BMW around the boy, careful not to scratch the mirror on the cars parked tightly on either side of the narrow street.

'And put some shoes on,' she shouted, pressing her foot to the accelerator.

Caryl had expected the house to look different. Aged, decrepit perhaps, but from the car it appeared the same. Cream window sills, grey pebble dash. The terracotta tiled doorstep that her mother had scrubbed weekly, the hard wire brush scratching away the street dust. She noted the addition of a black box on the wall below the doorbell. Her mother had had carers then. There was a handrail too, an ugly white bar that jutted out like an arm. No doubt her mother needed some assistance in her old age. Caryl wondered whether she had walked with a stick. She imagined her mother hunched over, her back a question mark. She'd have hated that.

Stepping out onto the street, Caryl made sure to lock the car securely. She tested the handle twice to be sure. She was wearing a black suit, a white chiffon blouse. She stopped to check her reflection in the car window. She carried a bouquet of lilies. Their stigma were fat with yellow pollen, and she held them away from herself in fear of staining her expensive blouse. She paused on the doorstep and took a breath to steady herself.

'Here we go.' She knocked the letterbox three times, took a step back and waited.

From inside the house, Caryl heard hurried footsteps. A female voice called, 'Coming.' Caryl's heart beat a jig in her chest and, just for a second, she considered turning away. The brown front door swung open. A woman in her fifties stood in the doorway. Her hair was scraped back into a severe bun. She was wearing a black dress which hung too loosely on her small frame.

'You're late,' Angharad said. 'We were expecting the flowers an hour ago.' She reached out and took the bouquet of lilies from Caryl's hands. Surprised, Caryl let her take them. 'Is this it? I ordered a wreath,' she asked sharply.

'I think there's been some confusion,' Caryl stammered. She hadn't expected Angharad to speak so sharply to her.

'I definitely ordered one. White roses spelling "MAM",' she insisted.

'I'm sorry.' Caryl didn't know what else to say.

Angharad's face fell.

'You haven't brought it?' she asked frantically.

'No. It's me, Ange.'

Angharad's face flushed red, and then quickly paled to white. 'Caryl?'

Caryl nodded her head.

'Most people call me Carol now.'

Angharad raised her thin eyebrows.

'Well, I guess you'd better come in then,' Angharad said, turning quickly on her heel and walking down the passage. Caryl paused a second longer on the doorstep before stepping into her childhood home.

She followed Angharad along the passage, passing the closed door of the front living room. The deer-headed barometer which she and Phil had broken as children still hung on the wall. The deer had only one antler, the other lost to an enthusiastic game of football. The Anaglypta wallpaper had been painted a sickly shade of green which clashed with the brown carpet. Walking into the kitchen, Caryl expected it to be equally unchanged but, to her disappointment, it had been modernised. Gone was the dark wood panelling, the washing line strung between the coving heavy with drying underwear. Her mother's gas cooker had been replaced with a modern silver oven. Caryl was surprised to find herself disappointed. The kitchen table was the same though, its surface pockmarked with dents and cup rings. It was pushed up against the back wall of the kitchen meaning only one side of the round table was extended. It gave the table an unsteady appearance as though it had been propped up.

When she was a child, Caryl's seat at the table was at the far end. She had to crawl underneath to reach the chair and spent dinner times with her elbows pressed against the cold wood panels.

I'd never fit now, she thought, suddenly conscious of the belly that she'd tucked into her fitted pencil skirt. She breathed in, tried to stand up straighter.

'You look well,' Caryl offered. Angharad was standing at the kitchen sink, filling the kettle. She had abandoned the lilies on the kitchen counter. Angharad didn't reply, nodded her head to indicate that Caryl should take a seat.

'Tea?' Angharad asked.

'I'll have an Earl Grey, if you have one?'

'I don't,' Angharad replied, removing the lid from the tea caddy and dropping two tea bags into floral mugs. The sound of the kettle filled the small space, and Caryl watched the steam blanch the window. She had practised this encounter hundreds of times over the years, but in the confines of the small kitchen, the words deserted her. Caryl felt nineteen again, all the words she wanted to say to Angharad dying on her tongue.

Angharad broke the silence.

'He's not going to be happy to see you, you know?'

Caryl nodded her head, 'I know. But I had to come, Ange.'

It felt nice to say her name again, to share small pleasantries. Angharad placed the mug of tea in front of Caryl.

'She's in the front room, if you want to see her,' Angharad said.

Caryl took a big swig of tea. It was too hot and burned her throat on the way down.

'Yes. Let me just finish this,' she said, indicating the mug in her hand. Caryl was in no rush to see her mother.

The heavy curtains in the front room were pulled tightly closed. Caryl could make out the shape of the piano, long un-played, in the gloom. Neither she nor Philip had any talent for music. In the far corner was the outline of a single bed. Next to the bed was a chair with metal handles and the shape of a bowl suspended underneath. Caryl averted her eyes quickly. She felt like she had seen more than she should, like a naughty child caught peeking. Photo frames lined every free surface in the room. They ranged in size, and although it was too dark to make out the smiling faces in the photos, Caryl was sure that she wouldn't find a photo of herself in the crowd.

The coffin was placed underneath the window. In the darkness, it looked unnerving, as though it might suddenly spring open. Caryl was aware of her own heartbeat thudding in her ears. Bile burned the back of her throat. *This is it*, she thought. Too late.

Caryl walked over to the coffin and placed a hand on the wood. It was surprisingly cold.

'I'm home, Mam,' she whispered. 'I got your letter,' her hand reached into her blazer pocket. She pulled the letter out. Its edges were worn soft from folding and unfolding. Caryl unfolded it again and recited the handful of words that decorated the page.

Time to come home, bach, she announced to the room. Just five little words. A casual summons like the one Mam would bellow from the doorstep when they were late home for tea. She had hoped for more. An apology maybe, an admission, but those five words were all she had. She refolded the letter into a careful rectangle and tucked it back into her pocket.

'Who was at the door?' A gruff voice bellowed down the stairs. 'Don't they know that we're in mourning?'

Upon hearing the voice, Caryl steadied herself, took a deep breath. She paused, her hand on the door handle. Her brother was halfway down the stairs when he spotted her emerging from the front room. Phil was wearing a white vest and striped underwear. His suit was slung over his shoulder.

'You!' He pointed a shaking finger at Caryl. His eyes bulged.

Caryl put her hands up as if in surrender.

'Please, I don't want any trouble.'

Phil careered down the remaining steps and gripped his sister by the scruff of her blouse. Caryl felt herself pushed against the wall.

Phil had dropped his suit and it had tangled underneath Caryl's heels. Up close, Caryl could see the deep lines on his brother's face, the scratchy stubble under his chin that he had failed to catch with the razor. Thin red veins decorating his cheeks.

'What are you doing here?' Phil spat the words from between gritted teeth.

At that moment, Angharad emerged from the kitchen, clutching an iron like a weapon. 'Philip Rees, put your bloody sister down. Now.'

Phil paused with his fist half raised. Then, thinking better of it, he shoved Caryl into the wall, and released his hands. 'What the hell is she doing here, Ange?'

'Your mother wanted her here so that's that.' Angharad scooped the suit up from the carpet. 'Look at the state of this,' she exclaimed, dramatically brushing dirt from the jacket sleeve. 'You need to get dressed,' Angharad pointed to Phil.

'Well, I'm waiting for you to iron my shirt,' he retorted.

'It's hanging up in the kitchen.'

Angharad disappeared into the kitchen, her husband trailing behind her. Phil turned and glared at his sister before slamming the door after himself. Caryl stood awkwardly in the passage, unsure what to do. This was a mistake. She smoothed down her blouse and then rubbed the corners of the letter in her pocket for reassurance.

When the funeral cars arrived, Caryl watched from the pavement as the coffin was carried out. In the daylight, the box looked too small, too insignificant to hold her mother. Every doorstep of Parry Street was occupied with people. They bowed their heads as the coffin was slid into the hearse. The wreath that Angharad had ordered, white roses spelling MAM, had arrived with the hearse and decorated the top of the coffin. Without it, the box could be holding anyone, Caryl thought. She wondered whether the coffins were sometimes mixed up – one person buried under another person's name – then shook the thought from her head. Too morbid.

They agreed that Caryl would travel in her own car to the funeral. Well, Angharad had agreed it with Phil. There were empty seats in the family car, but it wasn't right, Phil insisted. Caryl didn't mind. The thought of being pressed close to her brother, of feeling his warmth as he occupied more of the seat than he needed, his legs spread in a power stance, made Caryl feel sick. As she walked back down the street to her BMW, Caryl felt a thousand eyes watching her.

The chapel was packed to the rafters. Mourners in black occupied every seat and spilled out into the porch. Caryl had to abandon the car on double yellow lines, and now she was late. She tried to press through the throng, but people turned and tutted, resisting her attempts to move towards the front. She recognised more faces than she could put a name to. Faint memories swirled around her brain. The room smelled like damp and Sunday school. Caryl found that she was able to remember the first lines to the Lord's Prayer without effort. She wondered how many people remembered her and felt suddenly exposed. Maybe I'm better at the back of the crowd, she thought. Safer.

Caryl didn't recognise the pastor who delivered the eulogy and for that she was glad. She had expected to see the old preacher, John Jones, standing at the pulpit, delivering his words about God like pointed arrows fired into the congregation. This new pastor was younger, his words well-rehearsed and sterile.

'Mair was a much-loved member of the community,' he declared. 'She was the founding member of all manner of committees and societies like the Women's Socialist Society, Pontyrefail Community Watch and the local dart league. It could be said that nothing would have happened in Pontyrefail without her involvement.'

A polite ripple of laughter spread through the crowd. The overhead projector flashed a photo onto the back wall of the chapel. Mair Rees, in her fifties, her hair carefully curled, a floral pinafore over her mid length skirt and fussy blouse. On her feet, she wore sturdy boots. She was laughing at the camera, a rolling pin held aloft in her left hand. Caryl's breath caught in her throat. The slideshow clicked on. Mair on holidays, lounging in a deck chair on the beach, Christmas celebrations, a glass of sherry pressed to her lips. A family photo – three people around the dining table for lunch. The projector clicked again. On the wall was a photo of Mair holding a placard defiantly, her shoulders squared to the police officer who attempted to wrench it out of her hands. In careful writing she'd printed the words: 'Coal Not Dole'.

Caryl felt the panic rise from her feet. She was suddenly very hot. She felt as though the other mourners were pressing ever closer, crushing her. She looked around frantically. No one was looking at her but still she felt watched. The pastor's voice dimmed to a distant drone. Blood pounded in Caryl's ears. She had to get out. As she pushed her way to the doors, the pastor's voice came back into focus.

'Mair is survived by her only child, Philip, and his wife Angharad.'

Caryl emptied her stomach onto the paving slabs outside.

Angharad folded herself down gracefully and sat next to Caryl on the curb. Caryl didn't ask how she'd managed to extract herself from the sea of black or what excuse she'd given Phil. Caryl turned the folded rectangle of the letter around and around in her hands.

'It was you, wasn't it?'

Angharad met her gaze, nodded her head once.

'I should have known really,' Caryl said. 'It's been thirty years. I should have known.'

Angharad reached across and put her hand on Caryl's shoulder.

'I hope he was worth it?'

Caryl shook her head, a small no.

'He left me in '91. I woke up one morning and he'd just gone.'

Caryl wanted so badly to lean into Angharad, but she resisted.

'I wanted to reach out so many times, but Mam made it clear. I was guilty by association. Plenty of people agreed too. Women crossing the road to avoid me, shunned in the shops. Everyone treating me as if it was catching. Like if you stood next to me, your husband would cross the picket, too.'

'She still loved you, you know,' Angharad offered. 'She didn't say it but that's pride for you.' Angharad reached into the pocket of her blazer and pulled out a photograph. Its colours were muted, the camera flash rendering the faces too pale. A family photograph – the four of them on the threshold of the house in Parry Street. Caryl looked down at an earlier version of herself, all slender limbs and awkwardness. In the photo, she was laughing, her eyes locked with Angharad's as though they were sharing a joke only they could understand. Phil was standing to Angharad's right, his arm slung possessively across her shoulder. From the top step of the house, Caryl's mother beamed. She looked just like she remembered her – her hair set perfectly, tabard on, ready to spring into action.

'I found it in her things. Tucked away like a secret. I think you should have it.'

Tears pricked at Caryl's eyes, but she wiped them away stubbornly.

'Thank you, Ange.' She placed a hand on top of Angharad's. In a different life, she would have placed a kiss on her cheek. 'I didn't think it would be this hard. Not after all this time,' Caryl said.

'That's the thing about scabs. Sometimes you don't know how much the wound will bleed until you've pulled off the hard shell, revealed the soft fleshy bit underneath.' Angharad squeezed Caryl's hand, unfolded herself from the pavement. 'I'd better get back,' Angharad gestured to the chapel doors, the funeral cars waiting like slick black beetles. 'Take care of yourself.'

Caryl didn't wait around for the wake nor did she follow the funeral cars to the cemetery to see her mother's coffin lowered into the ground. She couldn't stomach the thought of triangle sandwiches and small talk in the back room of the 'Stute. Not that she would have been welcome. She walked back to her car slowly.

Before getting in, she glanced at the paintwork to make sure it hadn't acquired any scratches – more from habit than concern. She took another look at the photo that Angharad had saved for her, then slid it into the sun visor. The drive out of the valley was mercifully quick, the mountain road unspooling before her, pushing her forward towards flatter lands, and the sea. Caryl didn't look back except to see the road sign for Pontyrefail growing ever smaller in the rear-view mirror.

Something about Weddings

by Julie Primon

Weddings: cheer and confetti filling the air, the couple's love reflected into their guests' eyes like a pink sunset catching the clouds. The way people who have never met before will beam at each other without a second thought, caught up in this shared sense of wonder. Only at weddings, Claire thinks. Who wouldn't want to be a part of that?

Harvey, apparently. She tested his resolve before she left this morning, asked if he was sure, mentioned that there would probably be some last-minute cancellations. Her cousin Ed would no doubt make room for him if he wanted to come (at least, she hoped he would). But no. Harvey said he had to work, and he turned away from her, her carefully done hair and her pretty new heels.

She doesn't know why it bothers her so much. After all, she and Harvey have been together for years, and she knows how he gets. Family gatherings – external obligations – all these things make him uncomfortable. He will show the emotional side of him to her (sometimes) but not to anyone else. She knows this about him.

And yet, try as she might, she can't let it go. It casts a cloud on the whole day; she struggles to be present, to pay attention. Her ex-boyfriend, George, is standing tall at the front – he's Ed's best man, of course he is, she should have seen it coming – and Claire finds herself staring at him, at his wife's impeccable hairdo, at their little two-year-old son standing up on the bench to peer at the guests. The life she doesn't have, the life she gave up on. At dinner she has to sit next to Aunt Sue for two hours and listen to her endless list of complaints. Every few minutes she reaches into her purse and checks her phone, but no message has come through. *Fuck you*, she thinks, downing her wine.

Then, at last, the meal is over. Fanning herself with her napkin, Claire weaves through groups of people absorbed in shouted conversations. It's hot for September, twenty-six degrees, according to the BBC: at seven in the evening, the room is still heaving. Lucy and Ed have had their first dance and now a quicker-paced song is on, beat echoing under her feet.

Claire's parents are on the other side of the room, talking to Ed's mother. She could join them, but instead she slips out of the crowd, looking for the toilets. Outside the reception hall is a smaller, quieter hallway, and at the far end two doors leading to the men's and ladies' rooms. As she walks past, the door to the men's flies open, narrowly missing her face.

'I'm so sorry! Are you all right?'

Just like in a film, she thinks: here is George, standing in front of her, the moment ripe with awkwardness. It has been ten years, after all.

'Claire. Hi.'

'Hello.'

He seems at a loss for words. If this were just any other day, Claire would do the work and breach the silence, smile at him, make him comfortable, but this thing with Harvey has made her mean. She stands as tall as her swollen feet and uncomfortable heels will allow and waits.

'How are you?' he says finally, meeting her eyes.

His face is so earnest that the fight leaves her instantly. She takes a deep, steadying breath.

'Good,' she says. 'Work is going well. I was promoted a few years ago, and I'm one of the agency directors now. It's a lot of pressure, but it's very exciting too.' She can hear herself saying all those boring things as though from a great distance. 'I'm in a relationship. Been a few years. He just – couldn't make it today.' God, it sounds like a lie, as if she is ashamed and trying to cover up her singlehood. 'What about you?' she asks quickly.

'I'm well,' he says carefully. 'Work is... all right. Same old. I got married a few years back. We have a son, Tommy. You've probably seen him running around.'

'Yes,' she smiles. 'He's very cute. Looks like you.' She has seen videos of Tommy before, on Facebook – Tommy on a swing, Tommy at the zoo, Tommy throwing a spoonful of broccoli mash on the floor. She may, perhaps, have watched them more than once.

'Thanks. He can be a little demon at times, but he's our little demon.' George's smile ripples all the way down to her stomach. Unlike her, he's largely unchanged, his dark hair perhaps on the long side, his mouth still fleshy, sensual. Their first kiss might have been yesterday, shards of sunlight shining off the canal, George's strong hand at the back of her neck.

'I'll let you get on.' She gestures to the ladies' room.

'Of course.'

He stands aside. His aftershave is the same, and memories surface as she walks past him. The two of them in bed, slanted afternoon light catching their legs, the press of his nose behind her ear. The place in her body that smelled most like her, he said. She wishes, briefly, intensely, that she could travel back to that time.

Then she is in the ladies' room, sliding into a cubicle. A narrow window, cracked open, lets in the summer night's air. Claire breathes deeply; the fragrance of grass is delicious. She pees and finds that she doesn't want to get up. This is a nice hiding place, the cool air brushing her nape. She leans her head against the tiled wall. How different would today have been, she wonders, if Harvey had put his work aside for once, and come with her? He can be charming when he wants to. She imagines him at her side, tall, handsome in his Armani suit, making Aunt Sue laugh at dinner. No one else can make Sue laugh.

There is an added pressure to weddings, now that Claire has turned thirty. Family members glance enquiringly at her ring finger; they coo at little children and ask, 'How about you?' She answers through her teeth, *maybe, soon, we're not sure*. None of your goddamn business. Perhaps the wedding magic is truly gone. What a depressing thought.

The breeze from the window is getting cooler. She stands slowly, careful with the draping of her dress. She feels dazed, as though she has been jolted out of a dream.

'Claire? Are you in here?'

Her mother. Claire's hand goes still on the door's lock. If her mother looks down, she will recognise Claire's shoes, perhaps her very feet and legs. Idly Claire wonders what that might be like, to know a body so intimately because you carried it inside yours, because you watched it grow, day after day after day, into its final shape.

'Claire?'

She holds her breath. It would be easy to say yes, come out of the stall, but her mother sounds drunk, too cheerful for Claire's mood. After a few seconds, heels click away, and the bathroom door closes.

Claire slips out of her stall and washes her hands. The water is briskly cold, a relief around her swollen, ring-less fingers. She examines her face in the mirror. The day's heat has flattened the volume and curls that the hairdresser teased into her straight red hair. Her make-up is in good condition, only the faintest trace of mascara under her eyes, which she must have rubbed in fatigue. She has inherited her father's nose, straight and imperious, and his round chin. Unsmiling, her face looks severe, judging; her colleagues often joke about it.

Instead of returning to the party, she goes through the door at the end of the hallway. Fields stretch up a hill on one side of the barn; on the other, the ground slopes down towards a little copse. The heat was brutal earlier, but now it's loveliness itself. The cool air reaches a tender hand across Claire's shoulders, her calves. With a sigh she takes off her heels and stretches her bare feet against the cold, near-wet of the grass.

'Nicer out here, isn't it?'

Turning around, Claire is startled to find George's wife, Mrs. Blonde Mannequin with the impeccable figure. She is holding a cigarette and has also slipped her shoes off. Without the heels, she isn't much taller than Claire.

'Yes.'

There's a silence; they're looking at each other, Claire wondering if the woman – Sandra, her name is Sandra, there's no use pretending she doesn't know it – knows who she is.

'Want a drag?' Sandra says eventually, offering the cigarette.

Harvey would disapprove.

'Sure,' Claire says. 'Thanks.'

It tastes different than she remembers, more nuanced. Sandra doesn't buy any old brand. Claire tries to remember how long it's been since she last smoked. Five, six years?

'You can finish it,' Sandra says. 'If George saw me with it, he'd freak.'

George. She must know who Claire is, then, if she's referring to him by name. Instead of replying Claire takes another puff, savours it. It seems to enhance her senses, to make the evening more fragrant, luminous.

'I like your dress,' Sandra says. 'I wish I could pull off something like this. No chance in hell my boobs could fill it.' She giggles, perhaps surprised that she's sharing this with a stranger. Claire laughs in response, rather delighted at the compliment, the confession, the turn of their interaction.

'They might look nice in a dress,' she replies, gesturing at her chest, 'but trust me, the back pain's not worth the trouble.'

Sandra gives a half-shrug. 'I know. But don't we all want what we can't have? I thought having a baby would make a difference, but the moment I stopped nursing, it was back to 38B.'

She takes a few steps, looking down at her feet, her toes rubbing against the grass. Her figure, highlighted by the sunset, would look at home on the cover of a magazine.

'Have you ever done any modelling?' Claire hates herself for asking.

Sandra tilts her head back and laughs. It's a great laugh, a little throaty, not the sort of high-pitched thing you usually get from Londoners. Claire finds herself liking her.

'God, no. I could never stay in place for five seconds. It used to drive my parents nuts, my dad especially. *Sit down, Sandra,* he used to say.' She lowers her voice in mock imitation. '*Will you just sit down and be quiet for a second? Your mother and I are trying to have a conversation.*'

'You're an only child?'

'Is it that obvious?'

Sandra lets her purse, which has been dangling from her wrist, slide to the floor, and cups her elbows with her hands. Tilting her head, she looks at Claire.

'I was hoping you'd be here today,' she says. 'I was curious to meet you. But George didn't want to introduce me.'

'Really?' Claire takes one last puff and crushes the cigarette on the ashtray lining the path.

'I don't know why.' Sandra shrugs. 'He can be a bit awkward at times. But I mean, how long has it been since you guys broke up? Nine years?'

'Ten, actually.' Claire feels a pinch at her heart, being reminded. What is she doing, yearning for him after this long?

Sandra makes a thoughtful sound. 'What do you think? He's gained a bit of weight, hasn't he?'

Claire laughs, thrown by the question. 'I didn't notice.'

'I bet not.' Sandra's smile is too knowing. Claire shifts her weight from one foot to the other.

Sandra glances at the side door and picks up her purse. 'Sod it,' she says, getting another cigarette out. 'I'm going to risk it.'

After lighting the fag, she takes a drag and looks at Claire.

'What was George like, then, when you knew him?'

A dangerous question. Claire sifts her memories, looking for one least likely to offend. Her time with him is tinted with nostalgia. 'He was very charming. Very kind. So different from most other boys, who were always trying to prove themselves, parading like cockerels. George seemed like he knew what he wanted. And he was quiet, strong.'

'Why did you two break up, if you don't mind me asking?'

Claire sighs. 'My friends thought he wasn't ambitious enough, that I could do better ... I let myself be convinced.' This is what she has been telling herself for years, the source of many regrets, but as she says the words out loud, she realises that they're not quite true. 'Well, and I think we were going in different directions, too. I was very young. Maybe I needed that time to find myself, or to... learn to spend time with just me.'

Sandra smiles. Her expression is almost tender as she blows smoke out to the side, and Claire feels a strange, unexpected connection to George's wife, a bond she hasn't experienced with the friends made in recent years.

'It's an important thing, that. Learning to be in your own company. I'm still working on that one.'

A few people come out of the barn, a group of the bride's friends, perhaps – their faces are unfamiliar. Claire and Sandra exchange a look; they pick up their shoes and purses and move away. There's a stone bench against the side of the barn, and they claim it.

'You ever regret breaking up with him?' Sandra asks, taking another puff.

Claire looks at her. There is something freeing about this conversation, the two of them barely knowing each other.

'Sometimes,' she says. 'My current partner, Harvey – he's a very different type of person. Business-like. He has those grand gestures every so often, and I know that he trusts me, that he loves me – but he's not tender or cuddly on a daily basis. I miss that about George.'

'Hmm.' Sandra smiles softly. 'Yes, that was one of the things that attracted me, too. The way he touched my hair, my neck. Doesn't happen so much nowadays. He spends a lot of time at work, and when he comes home the priority's Tommy, not me.'

Her voice is tight with emotion, not bitterness, Claire thinks, but a kind of sorrow. Lightly she touches Sandra's hand. 'Maybe it's just temporary. You're still getting used to this new normal, the way a family just... rearranges around a child.'

The other woman nods, slowly releasing a puff of smoke. She stubs her cigarette against the side of the bench. For a moment, they just sit in silence, watching the night fall, the vast expanse of the sky tinged with inky blue. Claire is thinking about families, about solitude, about the things that are worth fighting for and the way memory can trick you, make you believe something that never was.

'I should go back in,' Sandra says. 'George will need help with Tommy.'

'It was nice talking to you.' Claire wants to say something else, give Sandra her phone number, ask that they stay in touch, but as their eyes meet and Sandra smiles, she can tell already that it won't happen, that they're too old or too far apart for a ten-minute conversation at a wedding to blossom into friendship. George's wife slips her shoes back on and walks away with a little wave of her fingers. Watching her, Claire feels none of the jealousy from earlier – as if a spell has been lifted.

Her purse gives a little shudder on her lap. She doesn't need to look at her phone to know that it will be a message from Harvey, saying something oblivious and sweet about her dress, perhaps, and asking her how the day went. He will end the message with two x's, as he always does, even though it is so utterly unlike him. They're half the reason she fell for him, those two x's.

She stands slowly from the bench. Although she can feel the day's weight on her body, there is a lightness in her chest, too. A kind of soaring.

Maybe weddings have some power left to them after all.

Pearls Before Swine

by Tracey Rhys

Evelyn was sitting at a restaurant table, with the midday sun making a white fuzz of the horizon. She had a view of the Med to her left, a glass of crisp white in her hand, and a handsome fella for company. Gio was a big, animated seal of a man. He had the whiskers, the pleading eyes, a neat plumpness to his body underneath his baby pink shirt. His white chest hairs poked out at the neck. They'd met on the cruise. Three days in and they were dining together, twenty days later and they were almost married. He was a divorcée, originally from Rio, recently retired from a marketing company. She was a widow, until last year a mover and shaker of three make-up counters in Debenhams. But they'd hit it off immediately.

At the Oyster Bar, it was Evelyn who had ordered a plateful of oysters and winked. Gio had rewarded her with a generous laugh and a 'What are you up to, you naughty girl?'

When they arrived, swimming in their shells, Gio had boomed, 'You know what to do with it? You have to swallow it whole, like this!'

He slurped one down, a sheen settling across his lips.

Evelyn tried to follow but God, they were impossible. She gagged.

Reached into her bag for a tissue, ignoring the serviette, and having spat it out, lay it on the table beside her.

'Urgh. How those things could turn anyone on is anyone's guess,' she told her surprised companion.

Gio reached across to the offending lump and fished about for a second.

'What the hell is that?' she'd squealed. 'I would have broken a false tooth on it. The sheer size of the thing!'

'Oh my God, Evelyn, a pearl. We must hide it.' And he slipped it into his shirt pocket where it bled into the cotton like a leaky nipple.

Neither of them paid much attention to the main course, and they refused dessert, which was something Evelyn would never have dreamt of, but her gaze kept drifting to the little round protrusion in Gio's breast pocket and his right hand did too, as if he had a dicky ticker.

'Are you alright?' she hissed.

'Yes, I'm just... You know, we could be robbed.'

We, Evelyn thought to herself. *I know where this is going.*

They wound their way back to the dock through the little streets. On any other day, the leather shops would have drawn Evelyn close to their muskiness, but the ship was waiting, towering over the dock like an ugly birthday cake, and she wanted to be in its carpeted depths.

'Home sweet home,' Gio chortled as they made for the gang plank. She disliked the way he placed his palm at the centre of her spine as they walked, as if he were steering an unwieldy ship. She was aware of the swing of her skirt as she went. *Old woman crosses gangplank*, she thought. Her reflection threw back someone she wasn't expecting. She was recently ancient, she decided. She recalled the same feeling in reverse when she was twenty and surprised at being a young woman.

In Evelyn's cabin, which was the type without a porthole frequented by the economy traveller, low enough so that the ship's engines reverberated through your chest each night, Gio upturned their prize onto a midnight blue scarf that Evelyn had bought in Madrid.

'Look at it!' he moaned, thumbing it with love, as if it had been the last tooth in his head.

'Stop it. You're acting deranged.' Evelyn took it in her hand. It was a decent size – a little egg of a thing.

'What do you think it's worth?' He'd got right to the point, she noted.

'Enough. At least, to take another holiday.'

Gio threw himself back on the bed which wobbled like blancmange. 'Good. Come here.' He patted the mattress.

Evelyn folded her silk scarf over the little gem until she'd made a puffy parcel. Then she stood and gaped around the room.

'What is it?' asked Gio.

'I'm wondering where to put it.'

'In the safe, of course.'

'I suppose so. I'll do it once you've gone.'

'Don't you trust me?'

'I'm not good at trusting anyone.'

Gio blushed, as if he had been found out.

'You must trust your family.'

'Pfft! If they knew I had any money, they'd be planning my funeral.'

'Good God! I don't think I want to meet them!'

'Play your cards right, Gio love, and you won't.'

His seal eyes saddened at that.

'Really? ... And these are your *children*?'

'Sometimes I wonder where they came from, then I remember my ex-husband.'

'Oh, dear God!' Gio muttered in Portuguese. 'This is terrible, Evie.'

'Don't call me that, Gio. My husband used to call me that and I can't stand it.'

'Of course ... Evelyn. Evelyn! I'm sorry. Why don't I let you take a nap?'

'Yes. I'm feeling a bit stressed.'

'But why are you stressed? We were having such a nice time!'

She found herself pulling a face that used to be cute, once upon a time. It involved shrugging, widening her eyes and sticking out her bottom lip. She caught him staring at her in fascination and stopped.

'What does that mean?'

'What?'

He mimicked her face.

'Just ... poor me.'

He was sat up now, his knees giving loud, embarrassing clicks as he flexed each leg.

'Listen, it... it's not worth that much, you know – your pearl. A thousand at the most. You can get rings – pearls set in gold – for less.'

'Yes, well that's quite a lot of money to some, isn't it?'

At 4:00PM, Evelyn had a big straw hat on her head, a bag hooked over one shoulder (the evening's pills rattling around inside) and was striding the narrow hallways towards the lifts. As she went, she glimpsed herself in mirrors: precisely half as glamorous as she felt, an expression of mild exasperation on her face even when she felt none. She tried speaking at a child in a pushchair.

'Hello!' It was the voice she'd used before her retirement, at the L'Oréal counters in Debenhams, best for persuading the young mothers to buy anti-ageing cream. It always worked. The little boy's face crumpled into a knot.

Evelyn got out on Deck 11 and flip-flopped along to where Gio was lying with his eyes closed. White curls protruded from his open linen shirt; a thick gold curb chain pooled into the skin at the base of his throat. His shades were on, mouth open.

Evelyn leaned in close, felt his breath in puffs against her cheek. She placed a hand on his shoulder and said in a deep voice: 'Giovanni Roussenq, you are under arrest!'

He sprung up and exclaimed something in Portuguese. Evelyn laughed so hard she passed wind.

'Were you asleep?'

'My God, I was. You gave me the shock of my life.' He took off his glasses: those blue eyes.

'Why did you do that, you crazy woman?'

'I thought you were dead.'

'That's quite an insult!'

'Recently deceased, if that helps.'

He grinned at her, waggling a finger, 'Evelyn, you are back to your naughty self!'

She slipped off her elasticated skirt and plucked at the legs of her swimsuit; then reclined slowly to avoid jarring her bad hip.

'My God, earlier today: it was so odd, wasn't it?' He was leaning forward, squaring up for a big discussion.

She closed her eyes and muttered, 'Odd how?' '

The entire morning ... like a weird dream. What have you done with it ... the pearl?'

'I've got it safe.'

He cupped a hand to his ear, 'In the safe?'

'Yes.'

'What will you do with it?'

Oh, mind your own, she thought. Then she sighed, 'Maybe a tiara.'

'That will be lovely, Queen Evelyn.' He kissed her shoulder.

She gave him a dirty look: 'I'm joking.'

'I know. Just don't let your kids get their hands on it.'

Evelyn had to glance away from him then, to pretend to concentrate on the untidy row of holidaymakers sprawled on the blue sunbeds, in various degrees of undress.

He touched the back of her hand and whispered, 'I think you're lowering the average age here to eighty-one.'

She laughed despite herself.

'One of them is meeting me, actually – my family – when we reach Greece.'

'You mean one of your *criminal kids*?' He took off his sunglasses and leaned forward. 'Who?' he demanded. 'Who is this?'

'My granddaughter, actually.'

'Oh.'

'Yes, she's a good girl. Don't worry. Her father is serving ten years for burglary and um … something else. I forget.'

He rubbed his eyes. 'Evelyn, you want to know something? You are a real one-off.'

She blinked at him, offended. 'What does that mean?'

He found himself waving his hands nervously, 'Most people would, er … Feel a bit, um … Maybe my English…'

'There's nothing wrong with your English, Gio, as well you know.' She crossed her legs neatly at the ankles and pressed them together like planks. 'It's too late for that; he's almost fifty. What have I got to be embarrassed about? I did everything I could.'

'Of course! But of course, dear.'

For five minutes the two of them lay side-by-side in silence, staring up at the apparatus beneath the deck above: the unsightly cladding and iron pipes. A shower of chlorinated water sprinkled them.

'Don't you worry about people's opinions of you, Evelyn? That they might look down on you?'

'I don't give two hoots. Besides, I only tell people I trust.'

'So, you *do* trust me?'

'Well, sometimes I tell people just to shake them up a bit, especially if they're living in cloud cuckoo land.'

'I don't know what that means.'

'A fantasyland. The real world isn't pretty, is it? Look at us: on a retirement cruise in the middle of the ocean. In ten years' time we'll be in terrible shape, and that's if we're still here at all.'

'You're in very nice shape, from where I'm sitting. Beautiful even, if you would allow me that.'

'Gio, I'm seventy-two. I'm happy with *you've got all your own teeth*.'

'Have you?'

'No.'

'Nor me!' He loosened something with his tongue and waggled a small clutch of incisors.

'Oh God, put them back in!'

'A vampire,' he chortled, sucking them into place. 'You look younger than seventy.' He stroked her arm with a finger.

'Seventy-two. Are you younger than me, Gio?'

'Oh yes, I'm twenty-three.'

She slapped him playfully on the wrist. His skin looked leathery with tanning, laced with delicate webs. They linked fingers. They were the kind of hands that hadn't seen any gardening, she thought to herself: no sand and definitely no cement.

'Come on, how old are you?'

'I'm catching you up, dear, put it that way.'

'So, you're not going to tell me?'

'I'll break it to you over a drink.'

'Go on then,' she nodded.

He dropped his teeth onto his lower lip again. 'Blood?'

'Margarita.'

He was sixty-five. She didn't know why it bothered her, but it did. He was a young man, by her standards.

'Are you after my money?' she'd asked him that afternoon. He'd been sat next to her, huddled in close.

'Evelyn, what do you take me for?'

'Off the top of my head, one of those honey-pot crooks, perhaps?'

'I'm insulted!'

'Only I don't have any money if that's what you're after.'

'I hope that's not true.'

He was looking quite sweaty, Evelyn noticed.

'I'm spending my last on this trip,' she told him, 'Every last penny.'

'And why would you do that?'

'To make some nice memories.'

'Oh my God, you aren't dying, are you?'

'We're all dying, Gio.'

'But ... Evelyn, do you have cancer or something?' He had fixed her with his most devoted of expressions.

'No.'

He seemed to relax, 'Thank God for that.' And he kissed her

cheek with a relief she found alarming. She finished her stupid cocktail; he ordered another beer from the bar.

In Santorini, they were grounded for most of the day. Evelyn's joints were inflamed from all the walking, so she and Gio hung back in a little roadside tavern near the sea, while he read out news stories from the paper.

'Ha! Listen to this!'

Oh God, do I have to? she wondered. The heat, the dusty road, the white and blue buildings rising high into an azure sky, the sea, even Gio's voice... She was in heaven, despite the pain.

'You don't need to stay with me,' she patted his hand.

'But I want to.'

'You should go, have a nice time.'

'I am!'

'I want you to bugger off for a while, Gio.' She smiled.

'Why?'

'I do. Go and have a nice day. Tell me about it. I'll see you later.'

'Are you sure?'

'Positive.'

'I feel like I shouldn't leave you here.'

'I'll be fine. I'm happy. See you in a few hours.'

He wandered outside with a certain uneasiness, his hands feeling inside various pockets as he went.

A teenage girl came out of the kitchen and greeted Evelyn with a kiss.

'Nanna!'

'My lovely.'

'Who was that, you dark horse?'

'Gio Roussenq. Your grandmother's latest squeeze.'

When they laughed, they made the same giggle.

'So, this is where you work?' The girl looked pleased. 'I've got something for you, Melissa. Look.' And Evelyn dropped the little bead of perfection into her granddaughter's palm.

'What's that?'

'A pearl. Not a pretend one, or even a cultured one. This is a real one, from a sea oyster.'

'Oh, wow!'

'Do you like it?'

'I do!'

'You can get it made into something.'

'Do you have the other one, Nan? I can get them made into earrings then.'

Evelyn laughed before realising her granddaughter was serious.

'No, love. This is a once-in-a-lifetime find, this is darling. You might never have another one of these again.'

'Won't I?'

'Probably not.'

'Well, if I do, I'll have a pair. I'll have a look down the market, then I'll make them into studs.'

'No! Don't mix it up with a fake one. This is worth its weight in gold, this is.' Evelyn was holding it in between her fingers again, shaking it at the girl. 'Get it valued.'

'Oh, I get it. For selling on?'

'If you need to. Or to pass on to your own daughter one day. A family heirloom.'

'Yeah, right. I'm not having any kids.'

'So, do you want it or not?'

'What do I do with it again?'

'Just keep it.'

'Then what?'

'It's really special, this is, Melissa.'

'Pearls are bad luck,' came a woman's voice from the kitchen. She strode over. 'You can't give them away. You have to sell them.'

'What?'

'Yes! Everyone knows this! Bad luck. Was it given to you?'

'...Well, not really.'

'Then you are lucky. Sell it.'

'I've never been lucky before.'

'Give your grandmother a coin.'

Melissa fished in a pocket.

The morning that they docked in Rhodes, Evelyn woke in Gio's bed on the second deck. He had a balcony, and the light was streaming in, new and bright.

'Good morning.' He kissed the top of her head as she raised herself up from beneath his arm. 'All right?' he asked.

'Yes. Aching.'

'It's all the gymnastics of last night!' he chuckled.

'It is! I'm in bits today.'

He wrapped an arm around her.

'Was it worth it?'

'Of course.' Outside, the corridor was slamming and banging into life. Voices and feet echoed along it.

'Breakfast!' she announced.

'Evelyn, I've been thinking. I want to make that pearl into something for you.'

'Oh no, it's all right.'

'Come on. Let's do it today. I want to make it into something for you to keep. To remember us.'

'Gio, you are the first thing that's happened to me in thirty years, I'm not going to forget you.'

'Well, let me do it anyway. A gift.'

Evelyn opened her purse.

The jeweller's was a small place, set with glass counters and big watches. Gio stood at the counter sweating through the underarms of his white linen jacket. When it was his turn, he dug in his pocket and unfolded the silk scarf.

'I want you to set this in gold,' he told the assistant.

The salesman looked surprised. It was just a Euro, untarnished but plain.

'For better luck,' he said. 'Set it like a pearl.'

Author Biographies

Gosia Buzzanca is a writer working across genres to create immersive, rich and texturally unique pieces of work touching on themes of motherhood, childhood, class, memories and belonging. She was born in Poland and moved to the UK at the age of 19, eventually settling in South Wales where she now lives and works.

Chinyere Chukwudi-Okeh is an English and English Literature graduate from the University of Ibadan and the University of Lagos, respectively. She recently specialised in Creative Writing and graduated from Swansea University. Her reviews and essays have been published in Nation Cymru. Across Wales, she has been to schools and events, doing what she knows how to do; sharing her creativity through Spoken Word, writing workshops, teachings on Black History and Windrush History, Storytelling with drum/flute accompaniments and via other multiple channels. She is currently one of the two women selected by Honno for the compilation of an anthology of memoirs for women of African and Asian descent in Wales. She has been published in Nigeria by Parresia Publishers. Her story, International Sisi Eko became the title of a collection of short stories by students and lecturers of the Department of English, University of Lagos, published by Farafina Publishers in Nigeria.

She is currently working on her novel and a children's novel. Chinyere is married with three lovely children.

Ellen Davies is a writer from the Rhondda, south Wales. She has a BA in English Literature and an MA in Creative Writing from Cardiff University. Ellen's poetry pamphlet, *Accent*, was published by Cinnamon Press in 2015 and her poems have appeared in *Mslexia*, *The Lonely Crowd* and *Popshot Magazine*, among other publications. Ellen's short stories have appeared in *The Ghastling* and the crime anthology *To Cast a Long Shadow* (Honno, 2022).

Naomi Paulus was born, and had most of her formative experiences, in Swansea. She graduated with a degree in Philosophy from the University of Cambridge, after which she spent a year at the Cambridge Judge Business School learning some practical skills. At 30, she decided to start writing down thoughts as well as just thinking them. She won the 2021 Rhys Davies Short Story Prize and has contributed to the BBC Radio 4 series 'Short Works'. She has been longlisted for the Primadonna Prize three times and won their 2020 flash fiction competition. She runs a digital agency in London in her spare time.

Julie Primon is a French author, editor and translator. She holds a PhD in Creative Writing from Cardiff University, and the creative part of her thesis, a historical novel titled The Girl from Caorle, was longlisted for the Mslexia Novel Award in 2020. She writes poetry as well as prose and recorded her poem, 'Married', for the podcast Talking Ink in 2019. Julie enjoys exploring the dynamics of human relationships in her writing; she believes it is connections and exchanges between people that make life interesting. She teaches creative writing at UWE and enjoys nurturing and encouraging her students' writing. She lives in Cardiff with her husband.

Tracey Rhys is a Welsh freelance writer, editor and artist. She received a Literature Wales New Writer Award for her debut poetry pamphlet, *Teaching a Bird to Sing* (Green Bottle Press, 2016), which was longlisted for the Michael Marks Award in 2017. Her poetry has appeared extensively in journals such as *Poetry Wales*, *New Welsh Review*, *Planet: The Welsh Internationalist*, *The Lonely Crowd* and *Ink, Sweat & Tears*. Anthology contributions include *Poems from the Borders* (Seren), *Bloody Amazing!* (Dragon-Yaffle) *A470: Poems for the Road* (Arachne) *Gwrthryfel/Uprising* (Culture Matters) and *Land of Change* (Culture Matters). Her writing has featured in a public exhibition at the Senedd for Autism Awareness month, and in professional theatre as performance monologues for Winterlight Theatre. Tracey's fiction can be found in the anthology *Cast a Long Shadow* from Honno (2022). In 2020, Tracey won the Poetry Archive's 'WordView Now' competition. Tracey's work is forthcoming for 2023 in a new anthology on Welsh dialect poetry (Culture Matters), prose in an anthology about friendship (Lucent Dreaming) and poetry in an anthology marking the centenary of the discovery of Tutankhamen's tomb (Black Bough Poetry).

Silvia Rose is a writer born and raised in Eryri. She writes poetry, prose and non-fiction, largely inspired by her Welsh and Serbian roots. In 2015 she graduated with an English Literature and Creative Writing BA from the University of East Anglia, then went on to run a film project in North Wales and set up her own English teaching business. Having recently returned home to the mountains after a time living in Granada, Spain, she now runs writing workshops and retreats in her local area and works as a creative freelancer. In 2021, she published her first poetry collection, *Spell into Being*, and is currently working on non-fiction projects. Her passions lie in fostering community, stories and folklore, and supporting creativity.

Carolyn Thomas was born in Neath and grew up in Tonna, a village in the Neath valley, among a close family where song, history, politics and poetry were part of everyday life. She has lived in Tyneside since her student days at Newcastle University and is now enjoying retirement after a career of teaching in Further, Higher and Adult Education. She has reviewed for *Stand* magazine and contributed poetry to the *Places of Poetry* online project as well as collections published by Sunderland University's Spectral Visions Press, an enterprise run by students studying English and Creative Writing. Her account of life as a gay woman in the 1970s was published in the Honno Press collection, *Painting the Beauty Queens Orange*. Stereotypically, she lives with a cat, still considers Wales as home and sports a dragon tattoo.

Kate Waddon is an 'unshakeably Welsh' Bangor-born freelance copywriter and parent to two teens. She lives in Penzance, writing anything from long-form to catalogue product descriptions. 'Wild Romances' came from people-watching at a service station. She has never abandoned her kids on the M5, however much they bickered over chips.

Editor Biographies

Rebecca Parfitt has worked in publishing for over 15 years. She has edited many short story collections and is also founder and editor of *The Ghastling*, a magazine devoted to ghost stories, the macabre and the strange. She is also a writer, poet and film-maker – her first short film, *Feeding Grief to Animals*, on her experience of miscarriage, was commissioned and produced by FfilmCymruWales and the BBC. Women and women's issues are at the heart of everything she does.

Mari Ellis Dunning is a poet and writer living on the west coast of Wales. Her poetry collection, *Salacia,* was shortlisted for Wales Book of the Year, while *Pearl and Bone* was selected as Wales Arts Review's Best Poetry Collection of 2022. She is a PhD candidate exploring witchcraft in 16th century Wales, and is founder of the Pay for Poets campaign. She is passionate about motherhood, violence against women and depictions of the female body.

ABOUT HONNO

Honno Welsh Women's Press was set up in 1986 by a group of women who felt strongly that women in Wales needed wider opportunities to see their writing in print and to become involved in the publishing process. Our aim is to develop the writing talents of women in Wales, give them new and exciting opportunities to see their work published and often to give them their first 'break' as a writer.

Honno is registered as a community co-operative. Any profit that Honno makes is invested in the publishing programme. Women from Wales and around the world have expressed their support for Honno. Each supporter has a vote at the Annual General Meeting. For more information and to buy our publications, please visit our website www.honno.co.uk or email us on post@honno.co.uk.

Honno
D41, Hugh Owen Building,
Aberystwyth University,
Aberystwyth,
Ceredigion,
SY23 3DY.

We are very grateful for the support of all our Honno Friends.